More Tales of Uncle Remus

FURTHER ADVENTURES OF BRER RABBIT, HIS FRIENDS, ENEMIES, AND OTHERS

More Tales of Uncle Remus
Further Adventures of Brer Rabbit,
His Friends, Enemies, and Others

as told by JULIUS LESTER

illustrated by Jerry Pinkney

DIAL BOOKS

New York

Published by Dial Books
A Division of Penguin Books USA Inc.
375 Hudson Street
New York, New York 10014
Text copyright © 1988 by Julius Lester
Illustrations copyright © 1988 by Jerry Pinkney
All rights reserved
Design by Jane Byers Bierhorst
Printed in the U. S. A.
W
10 9 8 7 6 5 4

Library of Congress Cataloging in Publication Data

Lester, Julius.
More tales of Uncle Remus. Further adventures of
Brer Rabbit, his friends, enemies, and others.

Summary: The author retells the classic Afro-American tales.
1. Afro-Americans—Folklore.   2. Tales—United States.
[1. Folklore, Afro-American.   2. Animals—Folklore.]
I. Pinkney, Jerry, ill.   II. Title.   III. Title: Further
adventures of Brer Rabbit, his friends, enemies, and others.
PZ8.1.L434Tal   1988   398.2'08996073   86-32890
ISBN 0-8037-0419-4 : ISBN 0-8037-0420-8 (lib. bdg.)

The publisher wishes to express its sincere thanks to the estate
of Joel Chandler Harris for its gracious support during the
publication of this new version of *The Tales of Uncle Remus*.

*Each black-and-white drawing is made of pencil and graphite; and
each full-color picture consists of a pencil, graphite, and watercolor
painting that is color-separated and reproduced in full color.*

To the memory of my father
J. L.

For my brothers and sisters,
Edward, William, Joan, Claudia, and Helen
J. P.

Who is Brer Rabbit? From where does he come? And why are these tales important? Since the publication of the first volume in this series, *The Tales of Uncle Remus: The Adventures of Brer Rabbit*, these are among the questions I've been asked most often.

These are important questions, reflecting both a curiosity about the mystery of folktales and our attraction to them, and a sense that these tales, as entertaining as they are, are more than entertainment.

Answering the questions entails dispelling some widely held and entrenched assumptions:

(1) Brer Rabbit is a symbol of how black people responded to slavery. Unable to resist physically, black resistance to slavery found sublimated expression through the figure of the wily Rabbit who outsmarted those seeking to oppress him. This is the interpretation offered by Joel Chandler Harris, who wrote that "the negro [sic] selects as his hero the weakest and most harmless of all animals and brings him out victorious." This view was reiterated by folklorists well into the present century.

(2) The Brer Rabbit tales were transplanted from Africa and are merely variants of the tales about Anansi the Spider, still current in West Africa.

(3) The tales are important because they chronicle the survival techniques used by slaves.

Such assumptions appear to answer the questions, but the appearance is deceiving. To accept these answers is to reduce the tales to imaginative political tracts. Such a view fails to recognize or appreciate the complexity and richness of Brer Rabbit. To see the tales only as the response of powerless slaves to slavery raises more questions than are answered. For example, if the Brer Rabbit tales are only a form of compensation necessitated by slavery, why have the tales always enjoyed a wide audience among whites? Most important, what is it in the tales that compels us to delight in the adventures of Brer Rabbit today?

The answer is simple: Whether we are black or white, slave or free, child or adult, Brer Rabbit is us.

2

Brer Rabbit cannot be explained by looking at his sociopolitical origins. If this were so, we might reasonably expect to find similar tales among many groups of oppressed people throughout time. What we find instead is similar tales among practically every people, regardless of the political circumstances of their lives.

Among North American Indian groups similar tales are found with the hero taking the form of Raven, Mink, Bluejay, Coyote, Rabbit, Hare, and Spider. Among blacks of the Bahamas and West Indies the figure is known as Compé Anansi, as Ti Malice in Haiti, and as Reynard the Fox in Europe. Whatever name a particular culture gives to this creature, he is the Trickster, or as the Winnebago Indians called him, "the cunning one."

How do we explain the similarities between Trickster tales? The famous tale of the "Tortoise and the Hare" is found in Aesop's Fables as well as the Uncle Remus Tales. It stretches credibility to believe that after a hard day's work in the fields, slaves sat around the hearth and read Aesop, especially since most were illiterate.

The universality of Trickster tales is not the result of cultural borrowings, but of the universality in what it is to be human. The emotions we live and the emotions which live us are culturally unbounded and are the same, whether enacted in a slave's cabin or in a king's palace.

The Brer Rabbit tales as collected by Joel Chandler Harris are rather tame for Trickster tales. They are even tame for Brer Rabbit tales collected by others, because Trickster tales are noted for their obscenity. ("Signifying Monkey" is a notable example in Afro-American folklore and is told today in many urban black communities.) Whether Harris never collected any of the obscene Brer Rabbit tales, suppressed them, or simply was unaware of them, we do not know. (In the famous "Brer Rabbit and the Tar Baby" story, there is only the minimal allusion in the Harris version that the tar baby is female. One can easily imagine a far more salacious rendition of the story in which the femaleness of the tar baby becomes central.) Despite the absence of the all-important element of obscenity in the Brer Rabbit tales as collected by Joel Chandler Harris, these tales share the essential characteristics of Trickster tales.

(1) Trickster tales do not have any feeling of "And they lived happily ever after." Instead we finish hearing or reading a Brer Rabbit tale fully aware that another tale has to follow. Indeed, we look forward to the continuation of what we sense to be and hope is an endless story.

(2) Trickster tales are not moral. Uncle Remus said, "Creatures don't know nothing at all about that's good and that's bad. They don't know right from wrong. They see what they want and they get it if they can, by hook or crook." The moralist in us may be outraged and offended by Brer Rabbit or any Trickster, because Trickster lies, cheats, deceives, and the reward for his trickery is not punishment but, generally, victory. We can enter the stories only by suspending "moral conscience," as Roger Abrahams, the eminent scholar of Afro-American folklore, phrased it. It is precisely in this suspension of moral conscience that Trickster is the avatar of a higher morality.

(3) Those who interpret the Brer Rabbit tales from a sociopolitical perspective point to the ingenious ways Brer Rabbit has of escaping the many plots of Brer Fox and Brer Wolf, who,

in this analysis, would represent white people. This analysis overlooks the fact that there are as many Brer Rabbit stories in which Brer Rabbit is the instigator of trouble, violence, and even murder. One notable example in this volume is "Being Fashionable Ain't Always Healthy."

While one might want to see Brer Rabbit as Victim, he is not. Neither is he Victor, because he is defeated more often than our image of him might want to admit. Trickster is beyond such a simplistic dichotomy, either pole of which would transform him into a cute bunny.

The outcome of Trickster's escapades is not crucial to the tales, nor important even. What is central is the spirit he brings to them. It is this spirit that both attracts and repels us. We envy it even as we shudder at the thought of emulating it. Regardless, we value Brer Rabbit's spirit, because, as Roger Abrahams wrote: "Trickster's vitality and inventiveness are valued for their own sake . . . the principle of vitality seems more important than that of right and wrong." What we value in Brer Rabbit and any Trickster is not only the amorality, but especially the raw energy of Life and Nature dramatized by the tales.

(4) The essence of Trickster tales is "patterned disordering," to use Roger Abraham's wonderful phrase. This is not the disorder which leads to chaos and destruction. Quite the contrary. It is disorder that is integral to the ordered pattern of life, that disorder without which life's ordered pattern would become rigid and sterile. It is the Trickster in us who knocks over the glass of water at a formal dinner. It is Trickster who makes so-called "Freudian slips," who laughs at the most inappropriate times.

Teachers and parents know Trickster well, because there is one in every classroom and every large family. Trickster is the class clown, the child who seems to have a genius for walking a thin line between fun and trouble, the child who is always "up to something," but you can never punish him or her because what he or she does is disruptive but never rebellious or serious enough to merit severe punishment. And it is always entertaining because Trickster is charming and likeable, surrounded as he or she is by an aura of innocence and vulnerabilty.

That Trickster tales should appear all over the world should not surprise us then, because Trickster existed before the tales. As the classical philologist Károly Kerényi put it, "The hero is stronger than the stories told about him. . . . [Trickster] comes before the expression in words. We must also grant him the greater consistency, an unchanging, indestructible core that not only antedates all the stories told about him, *but has survived in spite of them.*" (Italics added.)

Trickster would exist even if there were no tales. Fortunately there are tales, because "In mythology, we hear the world telling its own story to itself" (Kerényi). That is why we love Brer Rabbit. Through him we hear a portion of our story. It is not a story we could hear in any other way, perhaps because Trickster's amorality shames us. But "shameless untruthfulness is . . . a property of the world" (Kerényi), and therefore, a property belonging to each of us because we are human. To be moral about it does not always tell us how to live with it. Through the tales we live with, laugh with, and love, something of ourselves which is beyond our powers to redeem.

Trickster keeps us in reality. And this is where Trickster's amoral morality is superior to our moral posturing, our certitude that we know, absolutely, what is right and what is wrong. The more we are alienated from Trickster, the more likely we are to believe the inflated ideas we have about ourselves. Notice in the Brer Rabbit stories how often he exploits the other animals' images of themselves. Brer Rabbit appeals to their vanity, their pride, their posturing egos, and invariably they believe him. The instant they do, they are in Brer Rabbit's power and lost to themselves.

Trickster's function is to keep Order from taking itself too seriously. In Kerényi's words, "Disorder belongs to the totality of life, and the spirit of this disorder is the trickster. His function . . . is to add disorder to order and so make a whole, to render possible, within the fixed bounds of what is permitted, an experience of what is not permitted."

That is the charisma of Brer Rabbit, his undeniable appeal. Through him we experience "what is not permitted," and thereby we are made whole. Not perfect, but whole. The ideal of human perfection is one of the most dangerous of human delusions. To be human is to be whole. To be human is to love our irredeemable imperfections with the same passion as our virtues.

Károly Kerényi quotes W. F. Otto, who, in *Homeric Gods*, wrote that Trickster is the "spirit of a [lifestyle] which recurs under the most diverse conditions and which embraces loss as well as gain, mischief as well as kindliness. Though much of this must seem questionable from a moral point of view, nevertheless it is a configuration which belongs to the fundamental aspects of living reality, and hence, according to Greek feeling, demands reverence, if not for all its individual expressions, at least for the totality of its meaning and being."

Where others find it logical that the Brer Rabbit tales arose under the conditions of slavery, I think it is remarkable that they did so. The tales were not psychological compensation for the obvious lack of power in the slaves' lives. Rather, they represented an extraordinary effort to balance the totalitarian order of the slave system with archetypal disorder and thereby become whole.

We are not slaves, and yet the need for wholeness remains. I am awed that these tales about Brer Rabbit, created by slaves, speak so directly and with such clarity to us who are not slaves—that in these tales created by slaves is the vital voice of our humanity.

Julius Lester
Amherst, Massachusetts
16 September 1987

Contents

More Tales of Uncle Remus

FURTHER ADVENTURES OF BRER RABBIT,
HIS FRIENDS, ENEMIES, AND OTHERS

Brer Rabbit Gets Brer Fox's Dinner

If you ain't never heard about Brer Rabbit and Brer Fox, you might get the idea from these stories that they are enemies. Well, that ain't the way it is. On the other hand they weren't friends either. Brer Rabbit was Brer Rabbit, which meant he couldn't help it if he woke up some mornings and the first thing he thought about was creating devilment. And Brer Fox was Brer Fox. Wasn't his fault if he woke up thinking about the same thing. So they weren't enemies and they weren't friends. They were who they were. Another way of putting it is: They ain't who they wasn't. Now that that's all clear, let's get on with the story.

Not having anything better or worse to do one day, Brer Rabbit decided to see what Brer Fox was up to. As he got close to Brer Fox's house, he heard a lot of hammering. When he got there, he saw Brer Fox on the roof nailing shingles as fast as he could.

Well, Brer Rabbit treated work like he did his mamma, and he wouldn't hit his mamma a lick. So he looked around to see what else he could see, and there by the fence post was Brer Fox's dinner pail. Brer Rabbit knew there was more food in it than there was in his stomach. That didn't seem right. How was he going to get Brer Fox's dinner from where it wasn't doing no good to where it would do a whole lot of good?

"Brer Fox! How you doing today?" Brer Rabbit called up.

"Busy. Ain't got time to be flapping gums with you."

"What you doing up there?"

"Putting on a new roof before winter come."

"You need some help?"

"I do, but where am I going to get it at?"

"I'm a powerful man with a hammer, Brer Fox. I'll give you a hand."

Brer Rabbit climbed up to the roof and set to work. Pretty soon he was out-hammering Brer Fox. He was putting roofing on like winter was on the outskirts of town. He nailed and nailed and nailed until he was right up to Brer Fox's tail.

Brer Rabbit pushed the tail to one side, but, a tail being a tail, it just swished right back.

"Don't know how come some folks got to have such long tails," Brer Rabbit mumbled to himself.

He brushed the tail aside again and resumed nailing. He nailed under Brer Fox. He nailed around Brer Fox. He nailed beside Brer Fox. He nailed and he nailed until all of a sudden Brer Fox dropped his hammer and let out a yell, "Ow! Brer Rabbit! You done nailed my tail!"

Brer Rabbit looked at him, eyes big. "I done what? You got to be joking, Brer Fox. Don't be accusing me of something I ain't done."

Brer Fox hollered and squalled and kicked and squealed. "Have mercy, Brer Rabbit! Unnail my tail! Unnail my tail!"

Brer Rabbit started down the ladder, shaking his head. "I must be losing my aim, my stroke, or something. Maybe my eyes is getting weak. I ain't never nailed nobody's tail before. Doing something like that upsets me. Doing something like that upsets me so much, it makes me hungry."

All the while Brer Fox is hollering and screaming and squalling.

Brer Rabbit climbed down the ladder, still muttering to himself about how getting upset made him hungry. He opened up Brer Fox's dinner pail and helped himself to the fried chicken, corn, and biscuits inside. When he finished, he wiped his mouth on his coattail, belched a time or two, and went on down the road, hoping he hadn't done no permanent damage to Brer Fox's long, pretty tail.

Brer Rabbit and Brer Fox Kill a Cow

Brer Fox didn't have any hard feelings about getting his tail nailed, since no damage was done. So, a few days later, he and Brer Rabbit met up with each other, and after talking about first one thing and then the other they found out they had something in common: Their taste buds were crying out for some beef.

They went out to Mr. Man's field and killed his cow. I think it was Mr. Man's cow. Could've been Brer Porcupine's cow. Then again, it could've been Brer Snake's cow.

Then again . . . well, never mind. I know one thing: Brer Rabbit wasn't going to kill his own cow, and Brer Fox wasn't going to kill his.

They killed the cow, and Brer Rabbit told Brer Fox to run home and get a pan, tray, or something if he wanted the haslet. That's the liver, the heart, and innards. Some folks think there's nothing better. I don't happen to be one of them, but then again, I ain't in the story.

Brer Fox was crazy about the haslet, so off he went to get a pan. He couldn't get over the fact that Brer Rabbit would offer it to him. Maybe he wasn't such a bad fella after all.

As Brer Fox was thinking that very thought, Brer Rabbit was busy cutting out the haslet and hiding it in the woods. When Brer Fox came back, Brer Rabbit was sitting on the ground crying and boohooing.

"What happened, Brer Rabbit? What's the matter?"

"I wish you'd stayed, Brer Fox. I sho' wish you'd stayed."

"How come? What happened?"

"A man came and stole the haslet. I ran after him, but it must've been Fast-Foot Freddy. That sucker could run."

"Which way did he go?"

"Off down the road."

Brer Fox took off after him. Soon as he was out of sight, Brer Rabbit cut off the right hindquarter and hid it in the woods.

When Brer Fox came back, he was huffing and puffing and his tail was dragging the ground. He'd run almost to Los Francisco looking for Fast-Foot Freddy.

"You just a minute too late, Brer Fox!"

"What's the matter now?"

"Well, another man came along and took the right hindquarter. He went off through the woods over yonder. I know you can catch him 'cause he ain't got much of a start and he probably can't travel too fast carrying a hind-quarter."

Brer Fox took off again. Brer Rabbit cut off the left hindquarter and hid it in the woods. When Brer Fox came back empty-handed, Brer Rabbit told him that another man had come and taken the left hindquarter.

Brer Fox might be dumb, but even he had a limit. He looked kinna suspicious at Brer Rabbit but didn't say nothing. He pretended like he was going to look for this man but circled back and hid in the woods where he could see what Brer Rabbit was up to.

Brer Rabbit got busy butchering the forequarters and started carrying it off to his hiding place.

"Where you going with that beef?" Brer Fox demanded, jumping out at Brer Rabbit.

Brer Rabbit put the meat down, looked at Brer Fox, and shook his head in dismay. "Where you think I'm going with it? With all these men coming around stealing our beef I decided to hide this piece so we'd end up with a little something."

Brer Fox had had too many doings with Brer Rabbit to believe that. He grabbed at him, but Brer Rabbit ducked and took off running. They went through the woods, streaking like lizards going for a hole. Brer Fox was gaining on Brer Rabbit, but Brer Rabbit ran into a hollow tree.

"I got you now!" Brer Fox said.

About that time Brer Buzzard came along, and Brer Fox asked him to watch the hole while he went and got his carving knife.

"Brer Buzzard?" called Brer Rabbit. "There's a nice fat gray squirrel in here, and it's as dead as anything can be. It's just starting to stink, and I know you don't eat nothing that don't stink."

Brer Buzzard chuckled. "I don't believe you."

"That's all right, Brer Buzzard. I still got the advantage over you 'cause I can see you and you can't see me."

Brer Buzzard didn't think that was a good idea at all. No telling what Brer Rabbit would be up to if nobody was watching him. Brer Buzzard stuck his head inside the tree, and Brer Rabbit threw a handful of dirt in his eyes and ran out.

You think he ran home? Why would he do that? He ran back and got the beef he'd hid. Then he went home!

Brer Fox and the Grapes

Way back before "Once upon a time" and "In the beginning," there wasn't much difference between people and animals. That's the truth! You can see it on the face of a dog or cat to this very day. You know how a dog or cat looks at you sometime like it wants to say something? Well, somewhere along the way the animals forgot all the English they knew. So, when a dog or cat look at you like it wants to speak, it's trying to remember English, but it can't.

Reason I mention all that is because the animals went courting Miz Meadows and the girls, and I don't want to hear a whole bunch of nonsense about animals couldn't court ladies. What you learn in school is facts. What I talk is truth!

Brer Rabbit and Brer Fox were as crazy as they could be about Miz Meadows and the girls. If one wasn't sitting on the porch with 'em, the other one was. When Brer Fox came and found Brer Rabbit was already there, he would be so mad that he'd go down the road and bite off a sticker bush. Or when Brer Rabbit found that Brer Fox had beat him there, he'd go down the road a piece and paw up so much dirt, he'd find himself in a hole.

Brer Rabbit wasn't one to tolerate a situation like this for long, so he set himself to thinking about rectifying it. He was sitting alongside the road thinking and rectifying when Brer Fox come along looking as slick and shiny as if somebody had just taken him out of the box. Brer Rabbit hailed him, and Brer Fox stopped.

"Glad you come along, Brer Fox, 'cause I got some mighty good news."

"Tell it and be quick, 'cause Miz Meadows done invited me to dinner."

"Well, yesterday I came across the biggest and fattest bunch of grapes I ever seen. They were so big and fat that the juice was just oozing out."

Brer Fox's mouth started to water, and he forgot all about Miz Meadows and the girls. "Show me where they at!"

"I thought you said Miz Meadows put your name in the pot."

"Well, I can go see her and the girls later. Where them grapes at?"

Brer Rabbit squinched up his face. "Well, you know where you went to get sweet gum for Miz Meadows and the girls the other day?"

Brer Fox allowed as to how he did.

"Well, they ain't there. You go to the sweet gum, and then you go up the creek until you get to a patch of bamboo brier, but the grapes ain't there. Then you follow your left hand across the hill until you come to that big red-oak root—but the grapes ain't there. Then you go down the hill until you come to that other stream, the one with the dogwood tree leaning over it, and near the dogwood there's a vine. On that vine is the grapes. They so ripe they look like they melted together. You'll probably find them full of bugs, but you can take your fine bushy tail and brush them off."

Brer Fox thanked Brer Rabbit and he took off running. When he was out of sight, Brer Rabbit followed. Brer Fox didn't look to the right or the left, and he didn't look behind. He ran until he came to the sweet gum tree, and then he turned up the creek until he came to the bamboo brier and went to the left until he came to the big red-oak root and then down the hill to the stream where the dogwood was. He saw the vine. Way up on the vine were the grapes, and they were all covered with bugs, just like Brer Rabbit had said.

Brer Fox climbed up the vine and swatted at the grapes with his fine bushy tail. *Have mercy!* Brer Fox gave a yell that Miz Meadows and the girls said they heard all the way to their house. He yelled and—*kerblim!*—down he came.

Brer Fox learned a little too late that he was so busy looking at the grapes he'd pictured in his mind, his eyes forgot what a wasp's nest looks like. When Brer Fox fell off the vine, the wasp nest came too. Them wasps didn't like having their house knocked down, and they told Brer Fox a thing or two about it. He run and he kick and he scratch and he bite and he scramble and he holler and he howl, but the wasps wasn't through expressing their opinions on the situation.

Brer Rabbit was hid over in some weeds watching with great interest until the wasps made like they wanted to express their opinion to him, and he lit out and headed straight for Miz Meadows's.

When he got there, Miz Meadows asked him where was Brer Fox.

"He gone grape hunting."

Miz Meadows couldn't believe her ears. "Grape hunting? Me and the girls been in the kitchen all day cooking a nice supper for him. That's the last time he'll ever set foot on this porch."

Miz Meadows and the girls asked Brer Rabbit if he'd like to take supper with them, and he allowed as to how he would be pleased. He had just sat down at the table and tucked his bib in when he looked through the window and saw Brer Fox limping by. He was swollen up like a balloon about to bust. Brer Rabbit told Miz Meadows to look out the window.

Miz Meadows put her head out and hollered, "Brer Fox, you look like you ate *all* the grapes!"

Wasn't a thing he could do except slink on home.

_____

Brer Rabbit Falls in Love

One spring it was so pretty that folks who had never heard of love, didn't want to be in love, or had given up on it fell in love like it was a hole in the ground. Them kind of springs are dangerous. I reckon you too young to know what I'm talking about, but you will one day, and the Lord help you then.

It was one of them kind of springs when the breezes were so soft you wanted to grab one and put it on your bed to use for a sheet. It was one of them springs when the little leaves coming out on the trees looked better than money. Tell me that wasn't a dangerous spring! It was one of them springs when Brer Rabbit couldn't even think about causing no devilment. There ought to be a law against a spring like that!

Yes, Brer Rabbit had fallen in love, and it was with one of Miz Meadows's girls. Don't nobody know why, 'cause he'd been knowing the girl longer than black folks have known hard times, but that's the way love is. One day you fine and the next day you in love.

Brer Rabbit would go over to Miz Meadows and the girls in the morning, but instead of being full of stories and jokes like always he'd just sit there and sigh. Miz Meadows thought he had some dread disease like the rutabago or the Winnebago, especially when he started to lose weight.

Finally she asked, "Brer Rabbit? What's the matter with you? You sick?"

He hemmed and hawed and finally admitted that he was in love with one of the girls. He couldn't sleep, couldn't eat, couldn't steal, couldn't scheme, and was even beginning to feel sorry about some of the tricks he'd played on Brer Wolf.

"You sho' 'nuf in bad shape," Miz Meadows told him. "Have you told the girl you in love with her?"

Brer Rabbit shook his head. "I'm ashamed to."

Miz Meadows couldn't believe her ears. "Brer Rabbit, you *might've* felt something akin to shame before hens had their teeth pulled, but not since then. I done seen you do too many things to too many folks to be sitting here believing you feeling like you feeling. You can't convince me that there's a girl on the topside of the earth that could faze you."

"I'm ashamed to say it, Miz Meadows, but I'm afraid the girl won't have me."

"Just hush up your mouth and get on away from here. You ain't Brer Rabbit. You somebody look like him what's parading around low-rating his name. The Brer Rabbit I know wouldn't be carrying on like this."

Brer Rabbit couldn't help himself, and he went on off down the road until he came to a shade tree by the creek.

He hadn't been sitting there long before the girl he was in love with came up from the creek with a pail of water on her head, singing:

Oh, says the woodpecker, pecking on the tree,
Once I courted Miz Kitty Killdee,
But she proved fickle and from me fled,
And since that time my head's been red.

Brer Rabbit's heart started going pitty-pat, his ears jumped straight up in the air like attennae on a TV set, and he slicked down his hair real flat. When she finished singing, he sang back to her:

Katy, Katy! Won't you marry?
Katy, Katy! Choose me then!
Mamma says if you will marry,
She will kill the turkey hen;
Then we'll have a new convention,
Then we'll know the rights of men.

Now, don't be asking me what the last part of the song is about, 'cause I don't know. It was in the story when I got it, so I keep it. You can chunk it out for all I care.

By the time Brer Rabbit finished singing his song, the girl was standing there in front of him. She was a right pretty little thing, and she put down her pail and giggled at Brer Rabbit's song.

"How you this morning?" Brer Rabbit asked.

"I'm fine. How you?"

"Weak as water," Brer Rabbit said. "I ain't been feeling too well."

"So's I noticed. You got all the signs of somebody what come down with love. That's worse than the double pneumonia, TB, and terminal ugliness put together. The only cure is for you to go off somewhere and get a wife."

It was clear from the way she talked that she hadn't been

eyeballing him like he'd been eyeballing her, and that made him feel worse. He scrapped at the dirt with his foot, drawing little pictures in it. Folks do the foolishest things when they fall in love. Drawing dirt pictures with your foot! Finally he asked, "How come you don't get married?"

The girl bust out laughing. "I got too much sense than to do something like that without no sign or no dream."

"What kind of sign you want?" Brer Rabbit asked eagerly.

"Any kind! Don't make no difference to me. But I done tried all the spells, and I ain't seen no sign yet."

"What kind of spells have you tried?"

"So many I can't remember them all," the girl admitted. "I flung a ball of yarn out the window at midnight, and nobody came and wound it up. I took a looking glass and looked down the well. That was supposed to show me my future husband's face, but all I seen was water. I took a hard-boiled egg, scooped all the yellow out, and filled it up with salt and ate it without drinking any water. Then I went to bed, but I didn't dream about a blessed soul. I went out between sunset and dark and flung hempseed over my left shoulder, but my future husband didn't appear. Looks to me like I ain't gon' get no sign, and if I don't get a sign, I ain't gon' marry."

"If you'd told me about it, I bet you anything you would've seen your future husband."

The girl giggled. "Hush up, Brer Rabbit! If you don't get away from here, I'm gon' hit you! You too funny for words! Just who do you think I would've seen?"

Brer Rabbit drew another picture in the dirt with his foot, blushed, and finally said in a low voice, "You would've seen me."

The girl was shocked and hurt. "You ought to be ashamed

of yourself, making fun of me like that. I got better things to do than stand here and let you hurt my feelings." And she flounced on up the path.

Brer Rabbit sat down and thought that if that's how women were, maybe love wasn't all it was cracked up to be. But he was too far in love to know what good sense he was thinking.

He sat there for a long time, scratching his fleas, pulling on his moustache, and sighing. Suddenly he jumped up, cracked his heels together, and laughed so hard that he started choking.

"You want a sign, huh? Well, I'm going to give you one, girl! I'll give you a hundred!"

He went down to the canebrake and cut a long reed like the kind folks used to use for fishing poles. He hollowed it out and, when dark came, went up to Miz Meadows and the girls' house. He could hear them sitting around the table, laughing and talking.

"I saw Brer Rabbit down at the creek today," he heard the girl say.

"What was he doing there?" the other girl asked.

"I don't know, but his hair was slicked down and shining like glass."

Miz Meadows sighed. "I don't care nothin' about Brer Rabbit. I wish somebody would come and wash all these dishes."

The girls didn't want to hear nothing about no dishes. "Brer Rabbit said he wanted to be my husband. But I told him I wasn't marrying nobody until I got a sign. That's the only way I can be sure."

When Brer Rabbit heard that, he took one end of the hollow reed and stuck it in a crack on the outside of the chimney and then ran to the other end, which was laying in the weeds. He held it to his ear, and he could hear almost as good as if he was in the room.

Miz Meadows was saying, "Well, what kind of sign do you want?"

"I don't care," the girl answered. "Just so it's a sign."

Brer Rabbit put his mouth to the end of the reed and sang in a hoarse voice:

> *Some like cake and some like pie,*
> *Some love to laugh and some love to cry,*
> *But the girl that stays single will die, die, die.*

"Who's that out there?" said Miz Meadows.

She and the girls jumped up and hunted all over the house, all around the house, and all under the house but didn't see a soul. They went back in, and just as they sat down again, Brer Rabbit sang out:

> *The drought ain't wet and the rain ain't dry,*
> *Where you sow your wheat you can't cut rye,*
> *But the girl that stays single will die, die, die.*

Miz Meadows and the girls didn't know what to do this time, so they just sat there. Brer Rabbit sang out again:

> *I want the girl that's after a sign,*
> *I want the girl and she must be mine—*
> *She'll see her lover down by the big pine.*

Next morning, bright and early, the girl went down to the big pine. There was Brer Rabbit looking as lifelike as he did in his pictures. The girl tried to pretend like she was out taking a walk and happened to come that way. Brer Rabbit knowed better, and she did too. Pretty soon they was arguing and disputing with one another like they was already married. I suspect that was the real sign the girl had been looking for.

The Ol' African Helps Out

A new girl moved to town. Her name was Melody Mellif-ulous, and she was sho' 'nuf pretty. To tell the truth, she was fine! Brer Rabbit took one look, and his heart turned a double backflip and went *thumpty-thumpty, thump-thump.* He was weak in the knees, started trembling all over, and got light in the head. Some folks call that love. I calls it foolishness, which don't mean I ain't been foolish a time or two in my day. But that ain't part of the story, praise goodness!

Melody didn't care nothing about Brer Rabbit. He sent her flowers. She sent 'em back. He sent her greeting cards. She sent 'em back. He sent her a box of Swiss chocolates. She ate that. (Ain't no woman in the world gon' send back a box of chocolates.) No matter what he did, she didn't pay him no mind. If it had been raining and Melody had had the only umbrella in the world, Brer Rabbit would've drowned.

He was getting desperate, which meant there was only one thing to do. He went to see the Ol' African. The Ol' African was a conjure man. Folks nowadays don't believe in conjuring, and I feel sorry for 'em. Back in my time if you had a problem, you went to somebody who could conjure. The Ol' African was the best conjure person there's ever been. That man could get Kool-Aid out of a rock. One time he planted a garden, and while the rest of us was growing onions, tomatoes, and all like that, the Ol' African grew fried chicken, mashed potatoes, and gravy. If you was in trouble, that was definitely the man to see.

Brer Rabbit explained the situation to him. The Ol' African said, "You need a charm bag."

"Tell me what to do," Brer Rabbit exclaimed.

"You bring me one elephant tusk, an alligator tooth, and the bill of that bird called the ricebud."

"Be back in a little while," said Brer Rabbit.

He went way back out in the woods, and after a while here come Brer Elephant, busting through the trees big as Mt. Everest.

Brer Rabbit looked up at him. "You sho' are big. Something big as you can't be strong."

"Watch this," Brer Elephant said.

He grabbed a thirty-foot pine tree with his trunk, pulled it out of the ground, and flung it over his shoulder into the next county.

Brer Rabbit shook his head. "That tree was weak in the roots. I could see that before you pulled it up."

"Watch this!"

He ran through the woods and knocked over all the trees in his path.

Brer Rabbit shook his head. "Them was nothing but saplings. See that big oak tree? If you can destroy it, you strong."

Brer Rabbit pointed to a tree so big around, it looked like it had been growing since the Lord stuck it in the

ground. Brer Elephant ran into the tree and bounced off like a ball. He backed up, got a running start, and hit the tree again. He didn't bounce off this time 'cause one of his tusks was stuck. Brer Elephant pulled and he strained. After a while he realized that the only way to get free was to pull himself out of his tusk. That's what he did, and he sho' was a funny sight with only one tusk.

Brer Rabbit pried the tusk from the tree and took it back to the Ol' African. Ol' African said, "Elephant too big to be smart. Now I need that alligator tooth."

Brer Rabbit headed toward the creek, but before he got

there, he found Brer Alligator laying in the road, sunning himself.

"Ain't this road kinna inconvenient, Brer Alligator?" said Brer Rabbit. "You need a road what run right next to the creek. That way you wouldn't have to go so far to get in the water when you wanted to take a swim."

Brer Alligator liked that idea, so he and Brer Rabbit set to work. Brer Alligator was beating down the grass with his tail, and Brer Rabbit was knocking the bushes down with his cane. He hit left; he hit right; he hit up and he hit down and he hit all around. He hit and hit and he hit Brer Alligator in the mouth and knocked a tooth out. He grabbed the tooth and ran back to the Ol' African.

"Now I need the bill of the ricebud."

It took him a while to find a ricebud. It ain't one of your everyday birds, like a sparrow or a robin.

When he finally found one, he asked, "Can you fly?"

"Watch this!"

Ricebud flew up in the air, did a few loop-the-loops, and came back.

"That's pretty good," allowed Brer Rabbit. "But the wind have to be blowing when you fly. I know you can't fly when there ain't no wind."

They waited until the wind died down, and the ricebud flew around in circles, flew upside down, and did a couple of figure eights.

"You something else!" Brer Rabbit exclaimed when the ricebud came back. "But I bet you can't fly in the house when there ain't no wind."

Ricebud flew straight into the house, and Brer Rabbit shut the door. He caught him, pulled off his bill, and hurried back with it to the Ol' African.

Ol' African took the tusk, the alligator tooth, and the

ricebud bill and put 'em in a little bag. He put the bag around Brer Rabbit's neck.

"Melody Mellifulous won't be able to let you alone now."

That was sho' 'nuf the truth. She started sending Brer Rabbit flowers and cards and chocolate and begging him to marry her. But after doing all that work to get her Brer Rabbit wasn't interested no more. He finally threw the charm bag in the creek and Melody stopped pestering him.

The Courting Contest

I don't know what got into the animals, but they all fell in love with Miz Meadows and the girls at the same time. Now don't come telling me that a couple of stories ago you thought Brer Rabbit got married. That don't have nothing to do with nothing, 'cause animals ain't people and people ain't bananas. So, like I said, all the animals fell in love with Miz Meadows and the girls. Maybe somebody put something in the water, or Sister Moon turned up her lights too bright.

From sunup 'til moondown somebody was at the house. Especially around suppertime. It got so bad that Miz Meadows and the girls had to lock themselves in the bathroom to get a minute's worth of peace.

Miz Meadows got sick and tired of it! Seemed like the only way she was going to get rid of the animals was if she or one of the girls said "I do!" They weren't about to be that foolish. But they had to do something if they weren't going to spend the rest of their lives in the bathroom.

One Saturday morning Miz Meadows woke up, looked out the window, and Brer Rabbit, Brer Coon, Brer Possum, Brer Turtle, Brer Wolf, Brer Fox, and Brer Bear were sitting on the porch. Why, Brer Sun hadn't even finished his morning cup of coffee and there they were! And if that wasn't bad enough, she almost fainted from the smell of all the different colognes they were wearing. Enough was enough!

She stuck her head out the window and said, "Gentlemen, I have an announcement! Next Saturday I'd like y'all to meet me and the girls at the big granite rock down the road. The one who can take a sledgehammer and knock the dust out of it can choose which one of us he wants to marry. And until then I don't want none of y'all to darken my door."

Well, you ain't seen such excitement since us was freed from slavery. All the animals commenced to getting ready for the contest. They spent the whole week doing push-ups, sit-ups, chin-ups, and hiccups. They ran and jogged and skipped rope and lifted weights. All of them, that is, except Brer Rabbit.

He knew it was easier to get the wet out of water than dust out of granite. There had to be another way to skin this cat.

The night before the contest Brer Rabbit went over to Brer Coon's house and borrowed a pair of bedroom slippers. Next morning he filled the slippers with ashes from his fireplace, put 'em on, and went to the contest.

Well, when the animals looked around and saw Brer Rabbit strolling up with slippers on, they laughed. Brer Fox yelled out, "Say, Brer Rabbit! You forget to wash your feet?"

"Get out of my way," Brer Rabbit said, pushing the animals back. "I'm going to raise so much dust up out of this rock, Brer Sun won't be able to see nothing down here for a week!"

"Hold on, Brer Rabbit!" cried Brer Fox. "I was here first." He snatched the sledgehammer, reared back, and lammed the rock. Didn't knock a chip off it. He took two more turns and nothing. He was out of the contest.

Brer Wolf was next. He pounded on the rock three times real quick with all his might. He didn't get the time of day.

Next was Brer Possum. Didn't nobody expect much from him, and he didn't disappoint them.

Now came Brer Coon. Brer Coon made that ol' hammer ring, but he didn't raise no dust.

Brer Turtle's turn was next, but he said he had a crick in his neck.

Finally came Brer Bear. Miz Meadows and the girls got kinna nervous 'cause everybody knew if there was dust in that rock, Brer Bear would get it out. Brer Bear brought the hammer down; the ground shook. But no dust. He swung again; the trees shook. But no dust. The third time he hit the rock so hard the Lord looked down from heaven and hollered, "What you trying to do? Destroy the world?" Still, no dust.

Everybody got ready to go 'cause if Brer Bear couldn't do it, it couldn't be done. Miz Meadows and the girls breathed a sigh of relief. But they'd forgotten about Brer Rabbit.

"Hold on! Where y'all going? If y'all had let me go first, you wouldn't have had to embarrass yourselves."

He grabbed the sledgehammer, hit the rock, jumped in the air, kicked his heels together, and the dust from the ashes flew out of his slippers.

"Stand back, ladies!" He hit the rock again, kicked his heels, and dust flew everywhere.

"One more once!" he hollered. He hit the rock, kicked his heels, and there was so much dust in the air folks started coughing.

That was that. Brer Rabbit chose one of the girls for his wife, and they had a big wedding. I don't remember off-hand which one of the girls he married, but I think it was Molly Cottontail. Then again, it could've been Yolanda Yogurt. Ain't neither one a proper name for a lady if you ask me, but I guess in them days folks didn't know much about naming.

Brer Rabbit, Brer Coon, and the Frogs

Among the animals Brer Rabbit was the best at trickifying, but he had to share the title of best fisherman with Brer Coon. Brer Rabbit liked to set his line for fish, and Brer Coon liked to set his for frogs.

One summer, though, Brer Rabbit was having all the luck. He pulled in a mess of fish everyday, while Brer Coon couldn't catch a frog to save his soul.

"Brer Rabbit? How come you catching so many fish?"

Brer Rabbit shrugged. "I don't know. I just bait my hook, drop it in, and, before I can blink, I got a fish."

"I bait my hook, and I can't even catch a cold."

Brer Rabbit scratched his fleas. "You must've forgot about that time you made all the frogs mad."

"Me? What did I do?"

"You remember once during the dark of the moon when you caught King Frog?"

Brer Coon smiled. "He sho' was some good eating too."

"Maybe so. But ever since then everytime you show your face at the creek, I hear the frogs sing, *'Here he come! There he goes! Hit him in the eye! Hit him in the eye! Mash him and smash him! Smash him and mash him!'* That's what they say to one another."

"Well, if that's what's going on, how am I going to catch any of them? My family is getting so skinny, they navels are having long conversations with their backbones."

Brer Rabbit smiled. "Well, you and me been friends for a long time. You ain't never bared your sharp teeth at me, so I believe I'll help you out."

"Appreciate it, Brer Rabbit. I sho' do that."

"Tell you what you do. Get on that sandbar out there between the creek and the river. When you get out there, stagger around like you sick. Then whirl around and around and fall down like you dead. After you fall down, jerk your legs once or twice and lie still. And I mean still! If a fly lights on your nose, let him stay there. Don't blink your eyes; don't twitch your tail. Just lie there until you hear from me, and when I say move, you move!"

Brer Coon did just like Brer Rabbit told him. After Brer Coon had been lying there for a while, Brer Rabbit called out, "Coon dead! Coon dead!"

Frogs popped up from everywhere!

"Coon dead!" Brer Rabbit repeated. "Coon dead!"

One frog said: *"Don't believe it! Don't believe it!"*

Another frog said: *"Yes, he is! Yes, he is!"*

And a little bitty frog said: *"No, he ain't! No, he ain't!"*

The frogs got to croaking back and forth, disputing the matter. Brer Rabbit sat there on the bank scratching his fleas like he don't care what the frogs think.

The frogs decided to investigate and hopped over to Brer Coon. He looked dead. That he did. There was a fly crawling up inside his nose and he didn't even twitch.

Brer Rabbit called out, "Y'all been wanting to get rid of Brer Coon. This is your time, Cousin Frogs. Just bury him deep in the sand."

The Big Frog said, *"How we going to do it? How we going to do it?"*

"Dig the sand out from under him and let him down in the hole."

There must've been a hundred of them that went to digging. Sand flew out of so fast, it looked like a storm in the Saharry Desert. Brer Coon didn't twitch. The frogs kept digging until Brer Coon was in a nice hole.

"This deep enough?" Big Frog wanted to know. *"This deep enough?"*

"Can you jump out?" Brer Rabbit asked.
"Yes, I can. Yes, I can."
"Then it ain't deep enough."
The frogs made some more sand fly.
"This deep enough? This deep enough?"
"Can you jump out?"
Big Frog said, *"Yes, I can. Yes, I can."*
"Dig it deeper."
The frogs dug and dug and dug.
"This deep enough? This deep enough?"
"Can you jump out?"

"No, I can't. No, I can't. Come help me. Come help me."

Brer Rabbit laughed and hollered out, "RISE UP, BRER COON! RISE UP, AND GET YOUR MEAT!"

———————

Brer Rabbit's Laughing Place

Just like all the frogs got to disputing among themselves about whether Brer Coon was dead, the animals would get into disputes from time to time.

This particular day they got to arguing about who could laugh the loudest. Naturally each animal thought it could laugh louder than all the rest put together. Before you knew it, they were mad enough to fight.

Brer Bull broke in and said, "Tell you what we do! Let us have a laughing convention."

The animals liked that idea and said they didn't know Brer Bull had so much sense.

Brer Rabbit said, "Brer Bull ain't got no more sense than he ever had, and that was never much. Anybody with sense know that Brer Monkey is the laughingest thing on the top side of the earth."

The animals were embarrassed. The truth of that was so obvious they wondered why they hadn't thought of it.

"Anyway," Brer Rabbit continued, "what you need is a laughing place."

"What's that?" they wanted to know.

"A place that don't belong to nobody but you, a place where you can go anytime you want and laugh yourself silly."

"You got one?"

"Sho'."

"Well, how you know how to find a laughing place?" Brer Buzzard asked. "And how you know it's a laughing place when you get there?"

"Don't nobody have to tell you. You know."

"Can we see your laughing place, Brer Rabbit?" asked Brer Lion.

Brer Rabbit thought for a minute. "I can't be taking everybody to my laughing place. By the time y'all got through tromping around and laughing, wouldn't be no laughter left for me. But I tell you what. Y'all pick one body and I'll take him. He can come back and tell you what it's like."

The animals got to discussing it among themselves. Since each one of them wanted to go, everybody voted for himself, and another fight almost broke out. They figured the only way to solve it was to have Brer Rabbit choose.

"I pick Brer Fox," said Brer Rabbit. "He's highly thought of in the community, and I ain't never heard nobody breathe a breath against him."

The animals said that was a fine idea, and to tell the truth, they'd had Brer Fox in mind all the while.

Brer Rabbit told Brer Fox to meet him at Lucy's Crossroad that afternoon.

When Brer Fox got there, he looked around. "Don't look funny to me."

"Keep your shirt on, Brer Fox."

Brer Rabbit led him east-northeast-southwest until they came to a place where there were bamboo briars, blackberry bushes, and honeysuckles all tangled up together in a pine thicket.

"Now, what you got to do is run back and forth and

forth and back through the thicket."

Brer Fox didn't want to do it, especially since his wife had told him to watch out for Brer Rabbit. But Brer Fox knew if he didn't, Brer Rabbit would go back and tell all the other animals he was afraid.

So Brer Fox took a running start and went through the bushes and the vines like he was running a race. He ran around in circles; he ran around in squares; on one of them runs he made a trapezoid-triangle-square. He was having such a good time running that he didn't see the hornet's nest until his head knocked it off a low-hanging tree limb.

Them hornets jumped on Brer Fox with all their feet. He was running sho' 'nuf now and hollering yap, yap, yap, and ouch, ouch, ouch, and yow, yow, yow, and Brer Rabbit was laughing, laughing, laughing. Brer Fox rolled and wallowed and hollered and squalled and fell, and Brer Rabbit laughed and laughed and laughed.

After the hornets had enough fox meat to last 'em a while, they left Brer Fox sitting there in the thicket. He was so mad, he thought he was going to bust.

Brer Rabbit looked at him. "I'm sho' glad you had such a good time. I'll have to get you to come back again real soon. You looked like you was having a good time."

Brer Fox bared his teeth. "You said this was a laughing place."

"What you think I been doing, Brer Fox? Didn't you hear me laughing? I reckon you must not heard me right. I said this was *my* laughing place. Didn't say nothing about it being yours. And anyway, who ever heard of a fox and a rabbit having the same laughing place? Everybody know foxes don't have a sense of humor."

———————————

Brer Rabbit Gets the House to Himself

One time the animals were getting on so well together that they decided to build a house where they could all live. Brer Bear was there, and Brer Fox, Brer Wolf, Brer Coon, and Brer Possum. They were all there, even, as I remember, Brer Mink. They drew up the plans and set to work.

Brer Rabbit claimed that standing on a ladder made him dizzy, and if he stayed in the sun too long, he'd get a heatstroke. So he stuck a pencil behind his ear and walked around, marking this and that, measuring thems and thoses with a yardstick. Folks walking by saw Brer Rabbit and said he was doing more work than all the other animals put together. Of course, Brer Rabbit wasn't doing a thing and would've been more help if he'd just laid down under a shade tree and gone to sleep.

In no time at all, the animals had put up the finest house you've ever seen. It was two stories with a big curving staircase, forty-'leven bedrooms, seventeen-'leven bathrooms, a TV room, a room for video games, a sauna, a hot tub, central air conditioning, a Cuisinart in the kitchen, and a bidet for Miz Brindle and Miz Brune.

The animals moved in, and naturally Brer Rabbit took the biggest bedroom for himself. While the others were admiring the house and getting settled, Brer Rabbit went out and got a gun, a great big gun that would make a lot of noise, and sneaked it to his room. Then he sneaked in an old cannon, and finally a tub of nasty slop water.

The next day the animals were sitting in the TV room watching a soap opera. After a while Brer Rabbit excused himself and said he was going to go take a nap. The other animals didn't pay him no mind.

After a while they heard Brer Rabbit shout, "When a big man like me want to sit down, where he going to sit?"

The animals laughed and hollered back, "If a big man like you can't sit in a chair, he better sit on the floor."

Brer Rabbit hollered back, "You better look out then, 'cause I'm gon' sit down."

BANG! Off went Brer Rabbit's gun.

The animals got quiet. When they didn't hear nothing else, they went back to watching the soap opera.

After a while Brer Rabbit hollered out again, "When a big man like me want to sneeze, where he going to sneeze at?"

The animals laughed and hollered back, "If you such a big man, sneeze where you want to!"

"All right!" Brer Rabbit hollered back. "You better watch out, 'cause I'm gon' sneeze!"

And KABLUM! BLUM! BLUM! He set off the cannon. The windows rattled, and the house shook, and Brer Bear fell off his rocking chair—*kerblump!* Brer Mink and Brer Possum said that Brer Rabbit sho' must have an awful cold.

After a while Brer Rabbit called out again, "When a big man like me takes a chaw of chewing tobacco, where he gon' spit?"

The other animals were getting tired of this nonsense, and they hollered back, "Big man or little man, spit where you want to!"

Brer Rabbit hollered, "Well, this is the way a big man spit!" And with that he turned over the tub of slop water.

When the other animals heard it come sloshing down the stairs, they didn't get old and they didn't get gray getting out of that house. Brer Fox and Brer Wolf went through the front door. Brer Bear, Miz Brindle, and Miz Brune all tried to go through the back door at once, and that was a sight to see. Brer Otter and Brer Mink went through the windows. And the other animals went up and out through the chimney.

Soon as all the animals were gone, Brer Rabbit locked the doors and windows and went to bed, where he slept the sleep of the just.

Miz Partridge Tricks Brer Rabbit

You might be getting the impression that Brer Rabbit was the smartest thing that ever shined his shoes. He was smart all right, and sometimes when a person thinks he's so smart that he can outthink God, that'll be the time he finds out he ain't so smart after all.

One day Brer Rabbit had a yearning for bird's eggs. He got a basket, hung it on his arm, and set out. He was going through the woods, singing and humming to himself, when he saw Miz Partridge sitting in a hole in the ground.

"Where you going with that basket on your arm?" she wanted to know.

"Hunting bird eggs."

"Ain't that bad manners to be robbing a bird's nest?"

"When a man is hungry, he can't stand on manners."

"Well, if you want bird eggs, I'll show you some."

Miz Partridge took him to a nest with two big eggs in it.

Brer Rabbit looked and shook his head. "That's a hen's nest."

They went a little further, and Miz Partridge showed him a guinea nest. "Now, this is a sho' 'nuf bird nest."

"Ain't you got no sense, woman? This is a potrack nest. Let me do the leading this time. I'll find a bird nest."

Brer Rabbit headed straight for Miz Partridge's nest. She started getting nervous but thought her nest was hidden deep enough in the tall grasses that Brer Rabbit wouldn't find it.

Brer Rabbit stopped and sniffed the air. "I smell bird eggs."

Miz Partridge laughed nervously. "Can't nobody smell bird eggs."

"What you want to bet?" He charged through the grass, pushing it out of his way, until he found her nest piled high with eggs.

Miz Partridge pretended to be astonished. "My goodness! Who'd ever thought a body could smell eggs?"

Brer Rabbit started putting the eggs in his basket.

"Wait a minute, Brer Rabbit. You better let me examine them eggs. I done forgot more about eggs than you ever knowed."

Brer Rabbit couldn't argue with that. Miz Partridge broke one of the eggs open and tasted it. She hardly got it to her mouth before she fell over backward and started flopping and fluttering and twisting and turning. She flew up in the air; she fell down; she fluttered and jumped up again.

Brer Rabbit got scared. Miz Partridge was doing as good of a job of acting as Brer Rabbit had ever done.

"Run, Brer Rabbit! Run! These are snake eggs and they're poison."

Brer Rabbit ran away from there like Brer Dog was after him, and from that day to this a rabbit won't go near an egg.

The Famine

One year famine came to the community. The animals put their seed in the ground to make a crop, but the sky turned to iron and not a drop of rain fell. The leaves on the trees looked like they was going to turn to powder, and the ground was like it had been cooked. Old Man Hungriness had taken off his clothes and was parading around everywhere.

One day when the animals' stomachs were growling so loud they could barely hear themselves think, Brer Fox went to see Brer Rabbit.

"Where our bread gon' come from, Brer Rabbit?"

"Look like it might be coming from nowhere."

"I'm serious, Brer Rabbit. What we gon' do?"

They talked about the situation for a while until Brer Rabbit said, "Looks to me like we ain' got no choice but to sell our families."

Brer Fox nodded. "I think you right."

The next morning Brer Fox tied up his wife and put her in the back of his wagon and went over to Brer Rabbit's. He had his wife and all seven of his children tied up, and put them in the back of the wagon.

"I believe I'll set back here with my folks, Brer Fox, until they get used to the surroundings."

Brer Fox cracked the whip, and the wagon moved off toward town.

"No nodding back there," Brer Fox called out every now and then.

"You miss the ruts and the rocks, and I'll miss the nodding," Brer Rabbit would reply.

Brer Fox would chuckle. All the while, though, Brer Rabbit was untying his family. When he finished, he climbed on the seat next to Brer Fox, and they began talking about all the food they were going to get for selling their families.

After a while one of Brer Rabbit's children hopped out of the wagon, and Miz Fox sang out:

One from seven
Don't leave eleven.

Brer Fox turned around, kicked her, and told her to shut up that racket. Another of Brer Rabbit's children hopped out, and Miz Fox sang:

One from six
Leaves me less kicks.

Brer Fox didn't pay her no mind this time and went on talking with Brer Rabbit about all the food they were going to get. Miz Fox kept singing as the children kept jumping out of the wagon:

One from five
Leaves four alive;
One from four
Leaves three and no more;
One from three
Leaves two to go free;
One from one,
and all done gone.

When they got close to town, Brer Fox looked back in the wagon to make sure everybody was all right and saw that Brer Rabbit's family was gone. "Good grief! Where's your family, Brer Rabbit?"

Brer Rabbit looked and he began moaning and crying and screaming and wailing. "That's what I was afraid of," he hollered. "I knowed if I put them back there, Miz Fox would eat them up. I knowed it!"

Miz Fox swore up and down that she hadn't eaten them, but Brer Fox wasn't about to believe her. So when they got to town, he sold her, and he and Brer Rabbit went to the store and bought a lot of food.

They were on their way home when Brer Fox remembered that he'd forgotten to get some chewing tobacco. He asked Brer Rabbit to stay with the wagon while he hurried back to town. Brer Rabbit said he couldn't think of anything he'd rather do.

As soon as Brer Fox was out of sight, Brer Rabbit slapped the horses with the whip and took the wagon home. He put the horses in his stable, all the food in his smokehouse, the wagon in the barn, and some corn in his pocket. Then he cut the horses' tails off, went out to the road, and stuck the tails in the mud.

After a while Brer Fox came charging up the road. He was so angry the saliva was dripping off his teeth. Brer Rabbit saw him coming and started pulling on the horses' tails.

"Brer Fox! Run here! Quick! Brer Fox! You just in time if you ain't too late. Come here! Quick!"

Brer Fox ran to Brer Rabbit and shoved him away. "Looks like my horses done got caught in the quicksand. Get out of the way, Brer Rabbit. You too little and weak to do a man's job."

Brer Fox pulled hard on one of the tails. It came out, and Brer Fox went flying across the road. He jumped up and pulled on the other horse's tail. It came out, and he turned a somersault and went flying across the road again. While he was turning all these somersaults and flying across the road, Brer Rabbit sprinkled a little corn in the holes where the horses' tails had been.

When Brer Fox saw that corn, he started digging and grabbling in the mud and dug a hole deep enough to be his grave. And that's what it turned out to be too, because Brer Fox was digging so hard and so furious that he just plumb wore himself out and keeled over dead right there in the hole.

I tell you this much: It took Brer Rabbit and his family a lot less time to put the dirt back in the hole than it had taken Brer Fox to get it out.

Brer Rabbit, Brer Bear, and the Honey

All the animals—horn, claw, and wing—lived there in the community together, and they all shared the same fate. When times was good, they all prospered. And when times were bad, they all suffered.

When the famine came, it was one of the suffering times. Wasn't no food to be had, no money, and no jobs. It was all the animals could do to scuffle along and make the buckle and tongue meet. Most of them went to bed hungry every night.

All of them, that is, except Brer Bear. The skinnier they got, the fatter he got. He was just wallowing in fat. Shoots! Brer Bear was so fat, he couldn't keep the flies off himself.

Everyday the animals talked among themselves about how come Brer Bear was so fat and they were so skinny. Brer Rabbit was tired of talking and decided to keep an eye on Brer Bear.

Before long he noticed that Brer Bear was acting mighty strange. Instead of staying up at night talking politics and watching television, he was going to bed same time as the chickens and was up and gone by first light. It wasn't natural to go to bed with the sun and get up with it. If God had meant for folks to live like that, he wouldn't have invented electricity.

One night Brer Rabbit went over to Brer Bear's house. He scrapped his foot on the porch and cleared his throat. Miz Brune, and then again, it could've been Miz Brindle (I never could tell 'em apart)—one of 'em came to the door, and when she saw it was Brer Rabbit, she invited him in out of the evening chill.

Miz Brune pulled him a chair up close to the fireplace,

and Brer Rabbit crossed his legs and allowed as to how he hadn't seen Brer Bear in a coon's age.

"Times is so hard," Miz Brune said, "that my ol' man been working soon and late just to make both ends meet." She got up and said she had to fix a bag of ashes for Brer Bear to take to work with him in the morning.

"What in the world Brer Bear do with a bag of ashes, Miz Brune?"

She laughed and said she didn't know. "But I got to get a bag together every night and leave it for him in the corner by the chimney."

"Where is Brer Bear?"

"You sit here long enough, you won't have to ask where he at 'cause you be hearing him." She laughed. "I ain't never heard nobody snore like he do."

They chatted on for a while longer, and then Brer Rabbit said it was time for him to be getting on down the road. But he didn't go no farther than it took to find a place where he could hide and watch the house. He spent the night there, chasing lightning bugs and getting the frogs all confused by making frog sounds.

Long about the time the chickens started crowing up the sun, Brer Bear came out of the house, the bag of ashes over his shoulders, and made for the woods. Brer Rabbit followed along behind, but not wanting to get caught, he was scared to follow too close. First thing he knew, Brer Bear was out of sight, and for the life of him Brer Rabbit couldn't figure out which way he'd gone.

Brer Rabbit went home, worrying about what Brer Bear could be doing with a bag of ashes.

That night he went back to Brer Bear's house. After he was sure Miz Brune was good and asleep, he sneaked in and found the bag of ashes next to the chimney. He picked it up. It was sho' 'nuf heavy. He set the bag down and tore a tiny hole in one corner. Some of the ashes got up his nose, and he was about to sneeze. He held his breath and ran out of the house, and when that sneeze came out— goodness gracious!—the chickens started cackling and Sister Moon swayed for a minute like she wasn't sure she was going to be able to hang on to her perch. Brer Rabbit decided to get on out of there.

When morning came, he went back along the way Brer Bear had gone the day before until he saw a little trail of ashes. That was the reason he'd put the hole in the sack. Everytime Brer Bear took a step, he jolted the ashes out. Brer Rabbit followed the ashes, uphill and downhill, through bushes and through briars, until he came on Brer Bear.

Now, what you think Brer Bear was doing? If you said he was in a tree eating honey off a honeycomb, you would be right. He was eating the good stuff, the natural, stark-naked bee juice.

When Brer Rabbit saw him, though, he liked to have fainted, because Brer Bear had poured the sack of ashes over himself, and he was a horrible-looking sight. I reckon he'd covered himself with ashes so the bees wouldn't sting him. Brer Bear was way up in the tree, eating honey by the handful, with the bees zooming all around him. Brer Rabbit looked around, and everywhere were hollow poplar trees, and every one was so full of honeycombs that the honey was dripping down the sides.

Brer Rabbit watched Brer Bear eat honey until his stomach started saying *Want some! Want some!*

Brer Rabbit shouted up, "Please, Brer Bear! I'm awful

hungry! I sho' would be pleased if you'd hand me down a handful of honey."

"You better get away from here, you trifling, good-for-nothing cottontail nuisance."

"Please, Brer Bear! Just a handful."

"Get on away from here before I come down and make you into a pair of gloves for one of my children."

The next day Brer Rabbit got all the animals together—horn, claw, and wing—and told 'em how come Brer Bear was rolling in fat.

"Don't understand how he could do that to us," Brer Possum said.

"He could've at least let us smell some of that honey even if we couldn't taste it," said Brer Rat.

"Speak for yourself. I want me some of that honey!" said Brer Fox.

"And we gon' feast on honey before the sun start running from the moon," said Brer Rabbit.

"How?" all the animals asked at once.

"We gon' start a hurricane!"

If the animals hadn't known Brer Rabbit so well, they would've thought he'd lost his mind. But if Brer Rabbit said he was going to start a hurricane, a hurricane was coming.

Brer Rabbit led them quietly out to the honey orchard. He put all the big animals behind big trees and the little animals behind the little trees.

"Now, when I holler, y'all rub and shake these trees."

He told all the ones with wings and could fly to get up in the trees. "When I holler, you beat your wings as hard as you can."

All the ones with wings who could run but not fly high he put in the weeds. "When I holler, run through the grass as hard as you can."

When everybody was in place, Brer Rabbit took a long rope, and he went way back in the woods. Then he ran toward the honey orchard, dragging the rope and yelling and hollering.

Brer Bear looked down from the top of the tree. "What's wrong, Brer Rabbit?"

"Hurricane coming! Hurricane coming! I got to go somewhere and tie myself to a tree before I get blown all

the way to Jamoca Junction. Can't you hear it, Brer Bear?"
Brer Rabbit hollered real loud.

The animals behind the trees started shaking them, and
the birds in the weeds started running back and forth, and
the birds in the trees started fluttering, and it sounded like
the world was coming to an end.

Brer Bear scrambled out of that tree and hit the ground—
kerbiff! "Brer Rabbit! Tie me to the tree with you! Tie me,
too!"

The animals were into it now, and they were shaking
the trees and fluttering and running back and forth and
creating such a commotion that even Brer Rabbit started
to get a little scared. He hurried and tied Brer Bear real
tight to the tree, and when he tied the last knot, he called
to the animals, "Come and look at Brer Bear!"

All the animals came and laughed at Brer Bear, and then
they went to work on that honey orchard. They ate their
fill and then took a lot of honey home for their wives and
children. I expect that somebody came along eventually
and untied Brer Bear.

Brer Snake Catches Brer Wolf

The honey was good while it lasted, but it didn't last for-
ever, and it seemed like the famine was going to.

Brer Wolf and Brer Rabbit were talking one day.

"How is this here recession treating you, Brer Rabbit?"

"Not too good. Can't find a job. Ain't got no money,
and I'm hungry all the time."

"Me too. Me too," agreed Brer Wolf. "What can we do?"

Brer Rabbit shook his head. "I don't know, but something funny is going on. I saw Brer Snake yesterday. He was looking fat and sleek, while the rest of us are going around with our ribs showing. Seems to me that the country is in a bad way when our stomachs are growling so loud you'd think it was a thunderstorm, and the snakes are laying up in the sun like the economy was prospering."

"We ought to run all the snakes out of the country."

Brer Rabbit shook his head. "I'd rather find out where they getting their food from."

"Me too," agreed Brer Wolf. "Me too."

They decided to see what they could find out.

Next day Brer Rabbit was going through the countryside when he heard a noise in the woods. He jumped into a ditch and hid. A minute later Brer Black Snake come swishing by like he was greased. He swished on across the road and into the woods on the other side. Brer Rabbit followed at a distance and saw Brer Black Snake swish right up to a great big ol' poplar tree.

Brer Black Snake circled the tree one time, stopped, and sang out:

> *Watsilla, watsilla,*
> *Consario wo!*
> *Watsilla, watsilla,*
> *Consario wo!*

Before Brer Rabbit could blink an eye, a door in the tree flew open and Brer Black Snake swished in.

"I'll be!" exclaimed Brer Rabbit. "So that's where your food is."

Brer Rabbit went up to the tree to see if he could hear anything, but he couldn't. After a while he heard the same song:

> *Watsilla, watsilla,*
> *Consario wo!*
> *Watsilla, watsilla,*
> *Consario wo!*

Brer Rabbit leaped a leaping leap into the weeds, and as he did, the door in the tree flew open, and out swished Brer Black Snake. He looked around and then slid on his way. Brer Rabbit came out of hiding and went up to the tree.

He walked around the tree looking for the door but couldn't find it. Finally it came to him that maybe he had to sing the song.

> *Watsilla, watsilla,*
> *Bandario, wo-haw!*

As he sang the first part, the door opened a little ways, but when he sang the last part, it slammed shut. Brer Rabbit tried again:

> *Watsilla, watsilla,*
> *Bandario, wo-haw!*

Same thing happened. Door opened a little and then slammed shut.

"Must not have the song right," Brer Rabbit said.

Brer Rabbit went back and hid. That evening along came

Brer Black Snake again. Brer Rabbit crept closer as Brer Black Snake sang:

Watsilla, watsilla,
Consario wo!
Watsilla, watsilla,
Consario wo!

The door opened and Brer Black Snake swished on in. Brer Rabbit sang the song over and over to himself. Soon as Brer Black Snake came out and went his way, Brer Rabbit went up to the tree and sang the song. The door flung open and Brer Rabbit went in.

My goodness! He thought he'd died and gone to heaven. There was ham, pork chops, mince pie, fried chicken, hamburgers, and french fries stacked up in there hot, like they'd just been cooked. Brer Rabbit didn't wonder how and how come and all that. He just sat down and went to eating. When he'd had his fill, he went to tell Brer Wolf what he'd found.

Brer Wolf came back to the tree with Brer Rabbit. Brer Rabbit sang the song, the door opened, and he went inside, leaving Brer Wolf outside. After Brer Rabbit had eaten all he wanted, he came out.

"What'd you leave me out here for?" Brer Wolf wanted to know.

"You was standing watch. Now I'll sing the song and stand watch for you."

Brer Rabbit sang the song, the door flew open, and in went Brer Wolf. Brer Rabbit was standing watch until he heard Brer Black Snake coming, at which point he decided to keep watch from the bushes.

Brer Black Snake sang the song, the door flew open, and in he went. For a minute Brer Rabbit didn't hear nothing. Then there came all this noise, like a fight going on. The door flew open and out came Brer Wolf all tied up.

Brer Black Snake tied Brer Wolf to a tree limb and started wearing him out with his tail. And everytime Brer Black Snake hit Brer Wolf, Brer Rabbit hollered, "Serves him right! Serves him right!"

Brer Rabbit Gets the Meat

One day Brer Rabbit met up with Brer Fox. Now, don't come telling me about Brer Fox died a couple of stories back. What makes you think this is the same Brer Fox? Back in them times all the foxes was named Brer, and on top of that they all looked like one another too, which is how come they was all named Brer, 'cepting the ladies, of course. So, just because Brer Fox was dead don't mean he wasn't alive. Now, let me get back to the story before it melts and ain't worth telling.

"How you today?" Brer Rabbit wanted to know.

"Ain't doing too good. You?"

"Ain't doing too good myself. What's your problem?"

"Well, to tell the truth, I'm hungry. I can't remember the last time I had me a piece of meat. What's troubling you?"

"I'm hungry too. My stomach been having a long conversation with my backbone. I can't even remember what meat looks like, not to mention taste like."

They walked on together, commiserating and disputing about which one's stomach growled the loudest, when they saw Mr. Man coming toward them with a big piece of meat under his arm.

"Brer Fox! You see what I see?"

"Sho' do, Brer Rabbit! I wouldn't mind having a taste of that."

"We gon' get some of that meat. In fact, we gon' get all that meat."

"How, Brer Rabbit?"

"You just follow along behind me and Mr. Man at a distance."

Brer Rabbit hailed Mr. Man, asked after his health and the health of his family as he fell in step beside him. Mr. Man said that everybody was doing just fine.

"Glad to hear it, Mr. Man."

Brer Rabbit started sniffing the air like he smell smoke somewhere. After a while Mr. Man wanted to know if he had a cold.

"I smell something, and it don't smell like ripe peaches either," Brer Rabbit said.

Mr. Man said he don't smell a thing.

"Rabbits got better noses than people." Brer Rabbit kept sniffing the air until finally he grabbed his nose. "Peeuuu! Something just downright stinks!" Brer Rabbit looked around. "It's that meat you got, Mr. Man. Where'd you get that meat at? The dump?"

Mr. Man looked kind of ashamed, especially when he noticed some big green flies circling his meat. Brer Rabbit moved over to the other side of the road, still holding his nose. Mr. Man put the meat down.

"What can I do about it, Brer Rabbit?"

"Well, I heard that if you drag a piece of meat through the dirt, it'll get fresh again. I ain't had no experience with nothing like that myself, but my granddaddy said he tried it once and it worked."

"But I ain't got no string, Brer Rabbit."

Brer Rabbit chuckled. "You ought to spend more time in the woods and less in town. String ain't no problem." Brer Rabbit went off in the woods and, a few minutes later, came back with a long bamboo vine.

"That's mighty long, ain't it?"

"It got to be long," Brer Rabbit told him. "You want the wind to get between you and the meat."

Mr. Man tied the bamboo vine around the meat. Brer Rabbit broke off a branch from a bush and said he'd stay behind to fan the meat and keep the flies off.

Soon as Mr. Man started pulling the meat, Brer Rabbit got a big rock, untied the meat, and tied the rock on. Then he signaled Brer Fox, and they picked up the meat and ran into the woods.

Brer Fox suggested they sample it. Brer Rabbit couldn't have agreed more.

Brer Fox gnawed off a hunk, shut both eyes, and chewed and tasted, tasted and chewed, a silly smile spreading across his face. When he finished, he smacked his mouth, licked his lips, and sighed with satisfaction.

"That sho' is some mighty good lamb!"

"That ain't lamb," protested Brer Rabbit. "Any fool can see that that ain't lamb."

"It's lamb!"

"It ain't!"

Brer Rabbit gnawed off a hunk. He closed his eyes and

chewed and tasted, tasted and chewed, and then chewed and tasted some more. Then he smacked his lips, licked 'em real slow, and sighed with satisfaction.

"It's pork!" Brer Rabbit announced.

"Pork! Brer Rabbit, what's the matter with you? You ain't had meat in so long, you can't tell the difference between pork and lamb no more."

"It's pork!"

"It ain't!"

"Is!"

"Ain't!"

They argued and they tasted. They tasted and they argued.

"Well," Brer Rabbit began, "ain't no point in us arguing about it 'cause we can agree on one thing, I bet."

"What's that?"

"It's good!"

Brer Fox laughed. "That's sho' 'nuf the truth."

Brer Rabbit started walking away.

"Where you going?"

"To get a drink of water."

A few minutes later Brer Rabbit came back, wiping his mouth and clearing his throat.

"Where the stream at, Brer Rabbit?"

"Across the road, down the hill, and up the big gully."

Brer Fox went across the road and down the hill, but he didn't see a big gully. He kept going until he came to a big gully, but after looking all around he didn't see any stream.

While he was looking for the stream, which didn't exist, of course, Brer Rabbit dug a hole and he shoved the meat in and covered it up. Then he cut a long hickory switch and went and hid in a clump of bushes.

When he heard Brer Fox coming back, he took the hickory switch and hit a tree. *Pow! Pow!*

"Oh, please, Mr. Man!" he hollered.

Pow! Pow!

"Ow! Oh! Ooo! Don't hit me no more!"

Pow! Chippy-row-pow!

"Don't hit me no more, Mr. Man! Please don't hit me no more!"

Brer Fox was enjoying what he was hearing. It was about time somebody caught up to Brer Rabbit and gave him a taste of his own medicine.

After a while the racket died down, and Brer Rabbit hollered out, "Run, Brer Fox! Run! Mr. Man say he coming looking for you now!"

Brer Fox lit out from there. Brer Rabbit came out, dug up the meat, and let me tell you, he sho' did eat good that night.

Brer Rabbit Scares Everybody

The famine finally ended, and the next year Brer Rabbit made a good crop of peanuts. He sold it and was going to buy a red truck he'd had his eye on.

When he told Miz Rabbit what he was planning, she got righteous: "Truck, my foot! What you want a truck for? Where you gon' get the money to keep gas in it? Now you listen here to me, Brer Rabbit! The children need some tin cups to drink out of and some tin plates to eat off.

And I need a new coffeepot, 'cause you know how much I likes a good cup of coffee first thing in the morning. If you buy that truck, you best prepare yourself to eat, sleep, and go to the bathroom in it!"

Brer Rabbit had sense enough to know that he best back off on the truck. He smiled real nice, kissed his wife on the cheek, and told her he'd go to town Wednesday and buy up a whole lot of stuff for her and the kids.

Miz Rabbit didn't waste no time running across the road to tell Miz Mink that Brer Rabbit was going to town Wednesday to buy some nice things for her and the kids.

What she want to say that for? When Brer Mink got home that evening, Miz Mink told him what Brer Rabbit was going to do for his family, and she wanted to know when was Brer Mink going to do something nice for her? Miz Mink carried the word to Miz Fox, who proceeded to low-rate Brer Fox, and Miz Fox told it to Miz Wolf, who wanted to know from Brer Wolf how come he couldn't treat his family as good as Brer Rabbit treated his, and it didn't take no time at all for Brer Mink, Brer Fox, Brer Wolf, Brer Bear, and all the other animals to get together and declare that Brer Rabbit had gone a little too far this time. Playing tricks on folks was one thing, but buying your wife and children presents, well, that was something else again. They agreed very quickly to lay hold to Brer Rabbit on his way back from town that Wednesday and do away with him.

Wednesday came and Brer Rabbit went to town. He bought some soda pop, a plug of chewing tobacco, and a pocket handkerchief for himself. He bought his wife the coffeepot and a copy of Paris *Vogue,* and he got the children the tin plates, tin cups, and some *Star Wars* under-wear.

Toward sundown he headed home feeling mighty proud of himself. After a while he got tired from carrying all the packages and sat down under a tree to rest. He was sitting there fanning with one of the tin plates when a teenichy sapsucker started flying around his head chirping and carrying on. Brer Rabbit tried to shoo the bird away. The bird made more racket and finally lit right on top of Brer Rabbit's head and started singing:

> *Pilly-pee, pilly-wee!*
> *I see what he don't see!*
> *I see, pilly-pee,*
> *I see what he don't see.*

He sang it over and over until Brer Rabbit started looking around. Finally he saw marks on the ground where it looked like somebody had been sitting. He examined the marks a little closer.

"Well, well, well. There's the print of Brer Fox's tail. And there's the print of Brer Wolf's foot. And right there is the print of Brer Bear's bottom. They all been here, and I bet you anything they hiding out in the big gully down there in the hollow."

Brer Rabbit hid his packages in the bushes and slipped around through the woods to see what he could see. It was just like he figured. Brer Fox, Brer Wolf, and Brer Bear were hiding in the gully.

Brer Rabbit hurried back to where he'd hid his packages. He took out the coffeepot, turned it upside down, and put it on his head. Then he put the tin cups on his

suspenders and on his pants. Next he took the tin plates in his hands and sneaked back through the woods until he came to the hill overlooking the gully.

He ran down the hill—*rickety, rackety, slambang!* When the animals heard all the racket, they turned around. Never in their lives had they seen a creature with a coffeepot for a head and cups rattling all over his body.

Brer Bear jumped up, knocked Brer Wolf down, stepped on Brer Fox, and got away from there. Brer Wolf and Brer Fox was scrambling and trying to get up so they could get away, but before they could, Brer Rabbit was right on 'em.

"Gimme room! Turn me loose! I'm Ol' Man Spewter-Splutter with long claws, and scales on my back! I'm snaggletoothed and double-jointed! Gimme room!" And he jumped up—*rickety, rackety, slambang!*

Them animals tore up some trees getting away from there. Next morning Brer Rabbit went back to the spot, and he and his children picked up enough kindling wood to last through the winter.

Grinny Granny Wolf

Brer Rabbit went over to Brer Wolf's house one day and knocked on the door—*bim, bim, bim*. No answer.

"I know you there, Brer Wolf! How come you don't want to answer the door for me?"

Bam, bam, bam. Still no answer.

Brer Rabbit was insulted. "You better open this door before I knock it in." No answer.

Blammity-blam-blam-blam. No answer.

Brer Rabbit knocked the door down and went in. There was a fire burning in the fireplace, a pot sitting on the fire, and an old woman sitting by the pot. The fire was burning, the pot was boiling, and the old woman was taking a nap.

The old woman was Grinny Granny Wolf. She was cripple in one leg, blind in one eye, couldn't see out of the other, and deaf in one ear. But with her good ear she had heard Brer Rabbit banging on the door, and when he came in, she said, "Come and see your old grandma, Grandson.

The fire is burning; the pot is boiling. Come fix your grandma some food, Grandson."

She thought he was Brer Wolf.

Brer Rabbit made himself comfortable by the fire. "Hi, Granny! I'm crippled myself. I'm blind in one eye. I want you to boil me in the water. If you do, my leg will be well and I'll be able to see."

Brer Rabbit took a root and dropped it in the pot. "I feel all right now, Granny. My leg is getting strong and I can see out of my blind eye."

Grinny Granny Wolf cried out, "I'm cripple in one leg and blind in both eyes. Why don't you put me in the pot and make me well?"

Brer Rabbit laughed. "Why not, Granny? I'll make you all well again." He picked up Grinny Granny Wolf and put her in the pot of boiling water.

"Ow! Take me out of here!"

"Too soon. Too soon."

"I'm about to boil away. Ow! Take me out of here!"

"Too soon. Too soon!"

After a while she was dead. Brer Rabbit took the bones out of her body and left the meat in the pot. He took Grinny Granny Wolf's clothes and put them on. He took her cap and put it on. And then he sat in the chair she'd been sitting in.

After a while Brer Wolf came home. "I'm hungry, Grinny Granny. I've been working hard."

"Your dinner is ready, Grin'son Gran'son," said Brer Rabbit in Grinny Granny Wolf's voice.

Brer Wolf looked in the pot and smelled. He filled his plate and ate a big helping. When he was done, he patted his belly. "That was good."

Brer Wolf called his children to come have supper. The children said, "We can't eat our grandmama."

Brer Rabbit jumped out of the chair. "Brer Wolf, you ate your grandmama!" He laughed and ran on away from there before Brer Wolf could grab him.

Now, I tell you the truth: That ain't one of my favorite stories, but the way I look on it is like this: Brer Wolf must've done something sho' 'nuf terrible to Brer Rabbit for him to carry on like that. Something mighty terrible. Of course, if I sits here and thinks about some of the things been done to me and mine, I begin to understand that story more and more. I sho' do.

The Fire Test

Brer Rabbit had to go to town one day. He told his children not to open the door for anybody. Brer Wolf had been creeping around the house with big eyes and a angry belly, wanting revenge for what Brer Rabbit had done to Grinny Granny Wolf.

"When I come back, I'll knock on the door and sing:

I'll stay when you away,
'Cause no gold will pay toll!"

The little rabbits promised, and Brer Rabbit went on his way.

Brer Wolf had been hiding under the house and had heard every word. Soon as Brer Rabbit was out of sight,

Brer Wolf knocked on the door—*blip, blip, blip.*

"Who that?" the little rabbits called out.

Brer Wolf sang:

> *I'll stay when you away,*
> *'Cause no gold will pay toll!*

The little rabbits liked to have died laughing. "Go away, Brer Wolf! Go away! You ain't our daddy!"

Brer Wolf slunk off, but everytime he got to thinking about them tender young rabbits, his stomach growled. He went back to the door—*blap, blap, blap!*

"Who that?"

Brer Wolf sang:

> *I'll stay when you away,*
> *'Cause no gold will pay toll!*

The little rabbits thought that was the funniest thing they'd ever heard, even funnier than the last time Brer Wolf had come to the door. "Go away, Brer Wolf! Go away! Our daddy don't sing like he got a bad cold."

Brer Wolf slunk away, but a little while later he was back—*blam, blam, blam!*

"Who that?"

This time Brer Wolf sang as pretty as he could:

> *I'll stay when you away,*
> *'Cause no gold will pay toll!*

"Go away, Brer Wolf! Go away! Our daddy can sing pretty! Go away! Go away!"

Brer Wolf slunk off one more time. This time he went back out in the woods and practiced and practiced until he could sing almost as good as one of God's angels, which was almost as good as Brer Rabbit. He went back to the house, knocked on the door, and when the little rabbits asked who it was, he sang out so pretty that they opened the door. Brer Wolf rushed in and gobbled them up.

Toward sundown Brer Rabbit got home and found the door open. He went in slowly and looked around. He didn't see his children anywhere. He searched all over the house. Finally, over in the corner by the fireplace, he saw a pile of tiny bones.

Next morning he went to all the animals' houses and asked if they knew who had eaten his children. None of them did, especially Brer Wolf. Finally Brer Rabbit went and asked his best friend, Brer Turtle, what he should do.

Brer Turtle called a meeting of all the animals and made a proposal. "Now, somebody done gone and ate all of Brer Rabbit's children, and we got to find out who done it. If we don't, he might eat our children next, and before long won't be no children left in the community."

All the animals agreed with that, especially Brer Wolf.

"What we gon' do?" Brer Bear wanted to know.

"Let's dig a deep pit," Brer Turtle said.

"I'll dig the pit!" Brer Wolf offered.

"Let's fill the pit full of kindling and brush."

"I'll fill the pit!" Brer Wolf said.

"And then set it afire."

"I'll light the fire!" Brer Wolf offered.

"And when the fire is blazing hot, all the animals must jump over it. The one what destroyed Brer Rabbit's children will drop in and get burnt up."

Brer Wolf suddenly looked like he had business at the other end of the county. But since he'd been the one with the most mouth, the animals gave him the shovel, and he started digging.

After a while the pit was dug, and it was deep. The kindling and brush were piled high, and the fire was blazing hot. The animals stared at it, their eyes big, waiting to see who would go first.

Finally Brer Mink allowed that he never did have an interest in Brer Rabbit's children. To tell the truth, he didn't care too much for his own. He got a running start and jumped on over. Brer Coon was next, and he sailed over without even getting singed. Brer Bear said he felt heavier

than he had in weeks, but he hadn't seen Brer Rabbit's children since the town carnival. He leaped over. All the animals jumped over high and clear, except Brer Turtle, and nobody expected him to jump 'cause it was well known he didn't like rabbit meat.

So it was Brer Wolf's turn. He was trembling and was most sorry now he'd dug the pit so deep and the fire so high. He took a great long running start. By the time he got to where he was supposed to jump, he'd worn himself out. He jumped and landed right smack in the middle of the fire. All the animals knew then who'd done the deed, and not a tear was shed.

Brer Rabbit Catches Wattle Weasel

The animals were working on some project or other— building a Frisbee factory or something like that. Everyday when they came to work, they put their butter in the springhouse. And everyday when lunchtime came, they found that somebody had eaten their butter. They hid it every place in the springhouse they could think of. Didn't matter. Everyday the butter came up missing.

They did a little detective work and discovered Wattle Weasel's tracks around the springhouse. So they decided to take turns keeping watch.

Brer Mink had the first turn. He watched and he listened. He listened and he watched. He didn't see nothing. He didn't hear nothing. But he kept listening and watching because the animals had decided that if Wattle Weasel ate the butter while one of them was supposed to be watching, that animal couldn't have any butter for the rest of the year.

Brer Mink watched and waited. He watched, waited, and listened so long that he started getting cramps in his legs and the rheumeritis in his ears, and that was just about the time Wattle Weasel popped his head in the door.

"Hey, Brer Mink! What's happening? You look lonesome. Why don't you come out and play hide-and-go-seek with me?"

Brer Mink knew Wattle Weasel couldn't steal the butter if they were playing. They played until Brer Mink was totally exhausted, not to mention just plain tired. He flopped down on the ground, and Wattle Weasel dashed in the springhouse and ate all the butter. When the animals came to get their butter and found it gone, Brer Mink's butter-eating days had come to an end.

Next to stand guard was Brer Possum. He hadn't been there long before Wattle Weasel sneaked in. Wattle Weasel knew that the one thing Brer Possum couldn't stand was being tickled. He walked up to Brer Possum and started tickling him in the short ribs. Brer Possum giggled. Wattle Weasel kept tickling him, and Brer Possum kept laughing until he was lying on the floor panting for air. Wattle Weasel ate all the butter in peace. That was the end of Brer Possum's butter-licking days.

It was Brer Coon's turn next. Wattle Weasel came in the door and challenged him to a footrace. Brer Coon loved to run, and off they went. They ran and ran until Brer Coon was so tired he couldn't twitch a toe. But Wattle

Weasel could. Back to the springhouse he went and ate up the butter. Brer Coon sho' was going to miss eating butter.

Brer Fox was next in line to watch. Wattle Weasel was afraid of him, and it took a while to figure out how to handle him. He went down to Mr. Man's chicken coop, let all the chickens out, and drove them up to the springhouse. When Brer Fox saw all them nice fat hens, he couldn't help himself, and he dashed out to grab as many as he could. Wattle Weasel went in and ate the butter. Brer Fox joined them that were going to be eating dry toast.

Brer Wolf announced that he was the man for the job. He was setting in the springhouse when he heard some talking outside.

"I wonder who put that lamb down there by the chinkapin tree, and I'd sho' like to know where Brer Wolf is," Brer Wolf heard somebody say.

Brer Wolf tore out the door and headed for the chinkapin tree. When he got there, no lamb was in sight, and when he got back to the springhouse, neither was the butter. So he got marked down.

The next day Brer Bear had hardly taken his seat before Wattle Weasel sauntered in. "Thought I heard you snorting in here, Brer Bear. How you today?"

Brer Bear didn't say a word but kept a close eye on Wattle Weasel.

"You got any ticks on you, Brer Bear?" Before Brer Bear could answer, Wattle Weasel began to rub Brer Bear's back and scratch his sides. When it comes to back rubs, Brer Bear is kinna like my wife. Give that woman a back rub and you can near 'bout get anything you want. Brer Bear just relaxed, grinned, and before long his snoring sounded like a bunch of airplanes going off to war. Wattle Weasel ate the butter. When Brer Bear woke up, he knew his butter-eating days were a thing of the past.

The animals didn't know what to do. They talked about it for a while and decided there was only one thing to do: Send for Brer Rabbit.

A delegation went over to pay a call on him. They laid out the problem, and it took some talking before he was convinced that this wasn't some trick to catch him. Finally he agreed.

Brer Rabbit got a long piece of string, went to the springhouse, and hid up in the rafters. He hadn't been there long before Wattle Weasel came creeping in. He looked around, didn't see anybody, and just as he started to nibble the butter, Brer Rabbit hollered, "Let that butter alone!"

Wattle Weasel jumped back like the butter had burnt his tongue. "Brer Rabbit?"

"Who else? You let that butter alone!"

"Let me get one little teenichy taste, Brer Rabbit."

"Let that butter alone, I said."

Wattle Weasel pretended like he didn't want the butter anyway and suggested that he and Brer Rabbit run a race.

"I'm tired."

"Let's play hide-and-go-seek, then," Wattle Weasel said eagerly.

"I'm too old for that."

They talked back and forth for a while about what they could do, and finally Brer Rabbit had a suggestion. "Let's tie our tails together, and then we'll see whose is strongest."

Wattle Weasel had never played that game before, so he was agreeable. They tied each other's tails to the ends of a string, with Wattle Weasel inside the springhouse and Brer Rabbit outside. Soon as Wattle Weasel started to pull, Brer Rabbit slipped the string off his tail and tied it around a tree. Wattle Weasel pulled and pulled and strained and strained. Finally he hollered out, "Come and untie me, Brer Rabbit. Looks like our match is a draw. I can't outpull you and you can't outpull me."

Brer Rabbit pretended like he didn't hear him. After a while all the animals came because they were afraid Brer Rabbit had gone into cahoots with Wattle Weasel, and they would have to worry about two folks taking their butter. When they got there, Brer Rabbit was sitting outside filing his nails with an emery board, and Wattle Weasel was inside, tied by his tail.

That was one time the animals appreciated Brer Rabbit for being smarter than they were.

Brer Rabbit and Mr. Man's Chickens

Mr. Man had the nicest chickens anybody had ever seen. They looked ready for the frying pan without even taking their feathers off.

When the animals saw Mr. Man's chickens, they got friendly with him in a hurry. Every Sunday they came over, and Mr. Man didn't have no more sense than to show off his chickens. He took the animals into the chicken yard, and it was all they could do to control themselves. Brer Wolf's jaw trembled like he had the palsy. Brer Fox drooled like a teething baby. Brer Rabbit laughed like he had the hysterics and ought to be locked up somewhere.

One night when the moon wasn't shining, Brer Rabbit decided to call on Mr. Man. When he got there, all the lights were out. The dog was curled up under the house snoring almost as loud as Mr. Man.

"Something's wrong," Brer Rabbit said softly to himself. "Everytime I come over here, Mr. Man takes me in the chicken yard and shows me his chickens. Wonder is something wrong with him. I bet something done happened and nobody told me about it 'cause they knew how sorry I would be. If I could get in, I could see if everything was all right."

Brer Rabbit walked around the house and peeped in all the windows but didn't see anybody. "I bet if Mr. Man knew I was here, he'd come out and show me his chickens. So I might as well go make sure that they're all right."

He went to the chicken house, and lo and behold the door was unlocked. Brer Rabbit grinned. "Mr. Man must've known I was coming and left the chicken house unlocked so I could go in and admire his chickens."

He went inside. "It's on the chilly side tonight, and I'm worried that these chickens might get cold and freeze to death. If I'd been thinking, I would've brought a bag with me, and they could've used it for an overcoat." Then he looked down at his hands. "I don't know what's the matter with me! I got a bag right here in my hands and forgot that I had it. The chickens are lucky that I brought it. They would've frozen to death out here tonight."

Brer Rabbit proceeded to fill his sack with chickens. He was amazed that the sack didn't get full until every one of Mr. Man's chickens was inside. He took the chickens home, and him, Miz Rabbit, and the little rabbits spent the rest of that night cleaning them.

"Let's burn these feathers in the fire," Miz Rabbit said when they were finally done.

Brer Rabbit shook his head. "Whole neighborhood would smell them. I got a better idea."

He put all the feathers in the sack and, the next morning, went off down the road to Brer Fox's house.

Brer Fox was sitting on the porch. They exchanged how-do's and all the pertinent news about their families.

"Where you going, Brer Rabbit?"

"If I had enough wind, I'd be going to the mill, but this sack is so heavy, I ain't sure I'm going to make it. I ain't strong in the back and limber in the knees like I used to be. To tell the truth, I'm on the downgrade." Brer Rabbit let the sack drop to the ground.

"What you got? Corn or wheat?"

"Neither," Brer Rabbit said like he didn't want to tell. "Just some stuff to sell to the miller."

"Well, what is it?"

Brer Rabbit looked around as if he wanted to be sure nobody could overhear him. "Promise you won't tell a soul?"

"Promise," said Brer Fox.

"I got a sack full of winniannimus grass. They paying nine dollars a pound at the mill."

If Brer Fox hadn't been awake before, he was now. He came down and lifted the bag. "Feels light to me."

"Of course it feels light to a big strong man like you. To a little fella like me that's a heavy load."

Brer Fox swelled up with pride. "Well, I'll tote the bag to the mill for you if you want, Brer Rabbit."

"I sho' do appreciate it, Brer Fox."

Off they went down the road.

"Tell me, Brer Rabbit. What do they do with winniannimus grass after it's ground up?"

"Rich folks buys it to make whipmewhopme pudding."

After they'd been traveling for a while, Brer Rabbit looked back and saw Mr. Man coming and he was coming fast! "Brer Fox? You 'bout the movingest man I know. You done plumb wore me out, and I needs a little rest. You go on and I'll catch up with you. If I don't, wait for me at the mill."

"You take all the rest you need, Brer Rabbit."

Brer Fox went on, and Brer Rabbit sat down beside the road.

Not too many minutes passed before Mr. Man came up. "Who's that up ahead with that sack on his back?" he wanted to know, and he didn't ask too politely either.

"Brer Fox."

"What's he got in that bag?"

Brer Rabbit shrugged. "He said it was some kind of grass he was taking to the mill to get ground. But I saw some chicken feathers sticking through the bag, so I ain't sure what's in there."

"That's the man I'm looking for," said Mr. Man. "I'm going to make him sorry that he even knows what a chicken is."

Mr. Man went after Brer Fox, and Brer Rabbit ducked around through the woods and followed.

"What you got in the bag, Brer Fox?" Mr. Man asked when he caught up to him.

"Winniannimus grass. I'm taking it to the mill to get it ground. The rich folks make whipmewhopme pudding from it."

"I ain't never seen no winniannimus grass. What does it look like?"

Brer Fox put the sack on the ground, opened it up. Just then a little gust of wind come up and blew chicken feathers so high in the air, it looked like snow was coming down.

Mr. Man yelled, "Whipmewhopme pudding! I'm going to whip you and whop you and make pudding out of you!"

He grabbed Brer Fox and whipped him and whopped him until Brother Sun was running over to the other side of the world to get away from Sister Moon, who was intent on marrying him. And Brer Rabbit just laughed and laughed and laughed.

The Barbecue

Mr. Man not only had some nice chickens, but he also had the prettiest garden you'd ever want to see. Everybody came to see it. Some looked over the fence and admired it. Some peeped through the cracks in the fence and ooohed and aaahed. Then, there was Brer Rabbit. He preferred starlight, moonlight, cloudlight, and nightlight.

So there was Mr. Man; there was Mr. Man's garden; there was Brer Rabbit; and finally there was nightlight. That's a powerful combination, and there was only one thing that could happen.

One morning Mr. Man went to admire his garden, and wasn't too much to admire. All the cabbage was gone. All the turnips were gone, the carrots and the mustard greens too. He was so mad that he almost didn't see the rabbit tracks in the dust. That was about the only thing Brer Rabbit didn't take with him.

Mr. Man called up his hunting dogs and set 'em out hunting for Brer Rabbit. Brer Rabbit hadn't made it home yet, and he heard the dogs yipping and barking, and he started running. He ran around in circles and triangles and trapezoids and got them dogs so confused they didn't know where they were.

Brer Rabbit flopped under a shade tree and started fanning himself, and before long Brer Fox came by.

"What's going on, Brer Rabbit? I thought I heard a lot of dogs barking."

Brer Rabbit shrugged. "Mr. Man is having a big barbecue down to the creek. I told him I didn't want to come, but he says I gotta and set the dogs to running me there." He shook his head. "It's a problem being so popular. If you want to go to the barbecue, just get out there in the road and start running, and the dogs'll run you right to it."

Brer Fox started dribbling at the mouth and took off down the road. He was hardly out of sight before Brer

Wolf came up. Brer Rabbit told him the news about the barbecue, and off he went. The dust from his feet hadn't settled before Brer Bear came along. Well, when he heard about Mr. Man's special barbecue sauce and the juice oozing out of the meat, he took off. Brer Rabbit was watching him wobbling down the road when here come Brer Coon, and Brer Rabbit told him about the barbecue, and he was off and running too.

Well, when the dogs saw all the animals running along the road, they forgot all about Brer Rabbit and took off chasing the animals, and who knows where everybody ended up.

And that just goes to show you: When you get invited to a barbecue, you better find out when and where it's at and who's doing the barbecuing!

Brer Alligator Learns About Trouble

One day Brer Dog was after Brer Rabbit. I don't know what the trouble was, but Brer Dog ran through the woods, down the gully, up the other side, and over the gully, over the hill, and down to the creek, where Brer Rabbit ducked into a hole in the creek bank. Brer Dog came to a screeching halt. He sniffed around for a while but couldn't find him. Finally Brer Dog gave up and left, feeling pretty good. He'd given Brer Rabbit a run he wouldn't forget for a long time.

After Brer Dog left, Brer Rabbit crawled out of the hole and flopped down on the bank. He was huffing and blowing, trying to get his breath back, when Brer Alligator swam over.

"What's happening, Brer Rabbit? How come you huffing and puffing so hard?"

Brer Rabbit sat up and shook his head. "I been having trouble, Brer Alligator. Brer Dog was running me."

Brer Alligator chuckled. "I done got fat on trouble like that. I be glad to hear Brer Dog bark if he bring me that kind of trouble." He crawled out of the creek and lay down next to Brer Rabbit.

"Hold on there, Brer Alligator. When trouble come visiting, he makes your sides puff, and your breath come so fast you can't keep up with it."

Brer Alligator twitched his tail, stretched, and laughed. "Nothing don't bother me. I catch shrimp. I catch crab. I make my bed when the sun is shining hot. Yes, Brer Rabbit, I enjoy myself! I be proud to see trouble."

"I wouldn't be too sure about that if I was you. Trouble come upon you when you have your eyes shut; he come on you from the side you can't see. He don't come on you in the creek, he come on you in the broom grass."

"If he do, I'll shake his hand and tell him howdy."

Brer Rabbit was getting a little angry. "You can laugh at me, but you won't laugh when trouble comes."

Brer Alligator began to get sleepy. He nodded off, and his head dropped down, down, down until the grass began tickling his nose. He woke up, coughing and sneezing so hard that he almost blew all the water out of the creek.

This was obviously not a good spot for a nap, so he crawled to a nice open place of broom grass. He stretched out, closed his eyes, opened his mouth, and was asleep, just like that.

Brer Alligator slept. Brer Rabbit watched. In a few minutes Brer Alligator started snoring, and Brer Rabbit was sorry he hadn't thought to bring his earmuffs. After a while Brer Alligator started twitching in his sleep, and Brer Rabbit knew he was dreaming.

"This day I'm going to make you know trouble," Brer Rabbit said to himself. *"I'm going to make you know trouble very, very well, Brer Alligator."*

And with that Brer Rabbit proceeded to set the broom grass on fire.

Brer Alligator was dreaming hard now. His tail was flopping, and his body was twitching, and the broom grass was burning, burning, burning. Brer Alligator started dreaming that the sun was very, very hot, that it was warming his back, warming his stomach, warming his feet. Brer Alligator twitched and squirmed. Suddenly his eyes opened, and all around him was fire, fire, fire.

He ran to the north. Fire! He ran to the south. Fire! He ran to the east and to the west. Fire and more fire! "Trouble, trouble, trouble! *Trouble, trouble!*"

Brer Rabbit yelled, "Hey, Brer Alligator! What you mean, trouble?"

Brer Alligator lashed his tail. "Oh, my Lord! Trouble! *Trouble, trouble, trouble!*"

"Shake his hand, Brer Alligator! Tell him how do!"

"Oh, my Lord! *Trouble, trouble, trouble!*"

"Laugh with him, Brer Alligator! Laugh with him! Ask him how his health has been! You said you wanted to make his acquaintance. Now you got to get to know him."

Brer Alligator got so mad that he dashed through the burning broom grass and scattered the fire, which got all on his back. He dove into the creek, and the water hissed 'cause he was so hot. His tail shriveled up, and his back shriveled up. And they've stayed shriveled up to this very day. That's the reason the alligator has bumps on his back and his tail.

Of course, I reckon it goes without saying that any possibility of friendship between Brer Alligator and Brer Rabbit ended that day.

Brer Fox Gets Tricked Again

Brer Fox and Brer Rabbit were walking down the road one afternoon when Brer Fox saw some tracks in the dirt.

"Hold up, Brer Rabbit! Looks to me like Brer Dog been along here and not too long ago."

Brer Rabbit looked at the tracks. "That track ain't fit Brer Dog no time in world history. If I ain't mistaken, these tracks belong to Cousin Wildcat. I ain't seen him since I was a little cottontail."

"How big is he, Brer Rabbit?"

"He's about your size, I reckon. I remember when I was just a young'un, I saw my granddaddy beat up on Cousin Wildcat so bad, it made me feel sorry for him." Brer Rabbit chuckled. "If you want to have some fun, Brer Fox, that's some fun!"

Brer Fox wanted to know what kind of fun Brer Rabbit was talking about.

"Simple. Just go tackle Cousin Wildcat and knock him around some."

Brer Fox scratched his ear. "I don't know. His tracks are too much like Brer Dog for me. And I ain' never had no fun with Brer Dog, and he done had a lot with me."

Brer Rabbit looked disgusted. "Brer Fox? I'd never have thought a man like you would've been scared."

Brer Fox couldn't admit he was scared, so he went with Brer Rabbit to find Cousin Wildcat. They followed the tracks up the road, down the lane, across the turnip patch, and down a dreen. Don't come asking me what a dreen is. It's in the story that they went down a dreen, so that's what they did. And after they went down the dreen, they went up a big gully.

Finally they found Cousin Wildcat.

"Hey!" Brer Rabbit called out. "What you doing?"

Cousin Wildcat looked at him but didn't say a word.

"Ain't you got no manners? We'll teach you some manners if you not careful. Now, answer my question. What you doing?"

Cousin Wildcat rubbed himself against a tree just like a house cat rubs against the leg of a chair. He still don't say nothing.

"Why you want to pester us when we ain't been pestering you? I know you! You the same Cousin Wildcat what my granddaddy used to kick and beat. I got somebody here who's a better man than my granddaddy ever dreamed of being! I bet he'll make you talk."

Cousin Wildcat bristled up, but he still don't say a word.

"Go on, Brer Fox! Slap him down! That's what my granddaddy would've done. If he tries to run, I'll grab him."

Brer Fox wasn't none too eager, but he started toward the creature. Cousin Wildcat walked around the tree, rubbing himself, but he still don't say nothing.

"Slap him down, Brer Fox! Slap him down! If he tries to run, I'll catch him."

Brer Fox moved a little closer, and Cousin Wildcat stood up on his hind legs, his paws in the air. But he still don't say nothing.

"Don't you try that old trick, Cousin Wildcat! You fooled my granddaddy that way one time, but you can't fool us. Begging ain't going to help you. Pop him one, Brer Fox! If he runs, I'll catch him."

Brer Fox saw the creature looking humble, sitting up like he was begging for mercy, and he took heart. He marched up to Cousin Wildcat, and just as he was getting ready to pop him one, Cousin Wildcat hit Brer Fox in the stomach.

Brer Fox hollered so loud, four trees fell down, and the pictures on everybody's TV sets got fuzzy and stayed that way for a week. Brer Fox hit the ground, his arms wrapped around his stomach.

"Hit him again, Brer Fox! Hit him again! I'm backing you up! If he tries to get past me, I'll cripple him! Hit him again!"

But Brer Fox just lay there and moaned. Cousin Wildcat turned and walked away like he was the king of the mountain.

Brer Rabbit ran over to Brer Fox. "You had him and you let him get away!" And he ran on home, laughing all the way.

Brer Rabbit and Brer Bullfrog

Brer Bullfrog was the biggest nuisance in the whole community. He is the man what invented staying up late and carrying on. All night long and every night long Brer Bullfrog and his kin were up talking and arguing and singing and carrying on something outrageous. All the animals moved out of the neighborhood to get away from him. Next thing they knew, here come Brer Bullfrog saying he was lonesome.

Every night when folks had just got sleep good, Brer Bullfrog would start up: *"Here I is! Here I is! Where is you? Where is you? Come along! Come along!"*

The only one who didn't care was Brer Rabbit. Anything that upset the other animals was fine with him. And to tell the truth, Brer Rabbit liked to be out and about at night. So between Brer Bullfrog bellowing all night long and Brer Rabbit laughing all night long, the animals gave up and learned to sleep as best they could.

Well, this particular time Brer Rabbit noticed that he was just about out of calamus root, and the only place where it grew was down near where Brer Bullfrog lived.

Brer Rabbit hadn't been gathering the root long when Brer Bullfrog started up. Brer Rabbit had never heard Brer Bullfrog close up before, and he decided right quick that a little bit of Brer Bullfrog's music would last a lifetime.

"Where you going? Where you going? Don't go too far! Don't go too far! Come back soon! Come back soon!"

Brer Rabbit didn't have no intention of coming back. He'd have to see how cooking tasted without calamus root.

"Be my friend! Be my friend!"

Brer Rabbit tried to ignore Brer Frog.

"Jug of rum! Jug of rum! Wade in here and I'll give you some!"

That got Brer Rabbit's attention. He liked a little taste of rum every now and then, so he went down to the edge of the pond to look and see if there was a jug of rum setting on the bottom. The water looked mighty cold and very deep. It was going *lap-lap,* and Brer Rabbit had about decided to leave the jug where it was when, suddenly, he was in the water! He never knew if he slipped, fell, or got pushed. But he did know that he was in the water. He splashed and kicked and spluttered and finally hauled himself out. Day-old dishwater looked better than he did.

He sneezed and he snozed and snozed and sneezed, and so much water was pouring off him, he looked like a rainstorm.

If that wasn't bad enough, he had to listen to Brer Bullfrog laughing. Brer Rabbit drug himself home to dry off.

The next morning Brer Rabbit went to work, and I don't

mean no job. He went to work keeping an eye on Brer Bullfrog. He knew that when winter came, Brer Bullfrog had to move out of the pond before it froze over. And the day Brer Bullfrog moved would be the day he wished he hadn't.

Every day, all day, Brer Rabbit followed Brer Bullfrog around. Finally, one chilly morning, Brer Bullfrog come walking along the path in his Sunday best. He had on a little soldier hat with green and white speckles all over it, a long green coat, white satin britches, a white silk vest, and shoes with silver buckles. He was carrying a green umbrella, and he put the umbrella cover on his tail to keep it from dragging on the ground and getting dirty.

Now, just a minute! Don't be telling me that frogs ain't got tails. They ain't got tails *now,* which is how come we got this story. Back before my great-granddaddy's great-granddaddy's mamma's time frogs had tails, and you're about to find out how come they ain't got 'em no more.

Well, like I was saying, Brer Bullfrog was coming along the path going to his winter place when Brer Rabbit jumped out in front of him. Brer Rabbit looked at Brer Bullfrog, trembled like he was scared, and scurried off in the bushes.

Brer Bullfrog laughed and decided to have a little fun. He shook his umbrella at Brer Rabbit and hollered, "Where's my gun?"

Brer Rabbit came out of the bushes with both hands up in the air. Then he turned and ran.

"Come here, you rascal! Let me give you the whupping you deserve!"

Brer Bullfrog chased after him, and Brer Rabbit led him to a hollow tree where he had hidden an ax. Brer Rabbit grabbed the ax and ducked out the other side. Brer Bull-

frog ran into the tree. Brer Rabbit went around the tree, and when he saw Brer Bullfrog's tail sticking out of the hole—*whack! whack! whack!*

Well, that just took all the starch out of Brer Bullfrog. He ain't been himself from that day to this. And from that day to this frogs ain't had tails.

———————————

Brer Rabbit Meets Up with Cousin Wildcat

About a week later Brer Rabbit was galloping down the road—*clickety-clickety, clickety-lickety*—when something dropped out of the sky and grabbed him. It only took his mind a twitch to realize that it was Cousin Wildcat, who had been sitting up in a tree when he heard Brer Rabbit lickety-clickety down the road.

Cousin Wildcat hugged Brer Rabbit right close. Brer Rabbit started to kick and squall. Cousin Wildcat rubbed his wet nose in Brer Rabbit's ear. A cold chill went up and down Brer Rabbit's spine.

"Brer Rabbit, I just naturally love you," he whispered in his ear. "You been fooling with me. Your granddaddy fooled with me. And it wasn't so long ago that you tried to put Brer Fox on me." He chuckled way down deep in his throat. "Brer Rabbit, I just naturally love you." He laughed again, and his long teeth grazed Brer Rabbit's ears.

"Look here, Cousin Wildcat. I didn't put Brer Fox on you. I thought you'd want him for supper. If you can't understand that, ain't no point in you and me being friends."

Cousin Wildcat wiped his nose on Brer Rabbit's ear, but Brer Rabbit kept talking.

"Tell the truth, Cousin Wildcat. During all these years have I personally ever pestered you?"

Cousin Wildcat thought for a minute. "Can't say that you have."

"I know I ain't, and what's more, I have done my best down through the years to help you out. Now, even though you jumped down out of that tree on me and scared me so much that I was afraid my cottontail was going to drop off, I'm willing to do you another favor."

"What's that?"

"There's some wild turkeys not too far from here. Let's go over there, and I'll shoo them in your direction. You lay down on the ground like you dead, and when the turkeys come to investigate, you can jump up and catch a whole slew of them."

When they got to the place, Cousin Wildcat lay down in the clearing and pretended he was dead. Brer Rabbit went and found the turkeys. It was Brer Gibley Gobbler and all his kin. Brer Rabbit got in behind them and ran 'em toward Cousin Wildcat.

The turkeys stopped when they saw Cousin Wildcat. They stretched their necks and looked at him. Some said he was dead. Others said he wasn't. They gobbled back and forth, but they didn't get too close.

Cousin Wildcat lay there like he was dead. The wind ruffled his hair, but he didn't move. The sun shone down on him, but he didn't move. The turkeys gobbled and gobbled and stretched their necks. Then they gobbled some more. They stood on one foot and then the other, but they kept their distance.

It was too much for Cousin Wildcat. He jumped at one of the turkeys. The turkey flew up in the air, and Cousin Wildcat ran under him. He ran at another turkey. It rose up in the air, and Cousin Wildcat ran under him. He kept running and leaping, and the turkeys kept flying up in the air until Cousin Wildcat was stiff in his joints, out of breath, and just plain humiliated. He fell over on the ground, and Brer Gibley Gobbler got his kin away from there.

And to this day when you hear turkeys gobbling, they be talking about what happened way back there in the ancient times when Cousin Wildcat tried to catch them.

Brer Rabbit Gets a Little Comeuppance

Once a year all the animals got together for their political convention. This was when they went over all their laws to see if any needed to be thrown out, or if they should make some new ones. They made highfaluting speeches and generally enjoyed piling words on top of words like they was afraid language was going out of fashion.

This particular year Brer Rabbit was sitting next to Brer Dog. Everytime Brer Dog opened his mouth to make a speech, Brer Rabbit couldn't help noticing how strong his teeth looked and how bright and white they shone. It made him kind of nervous.

Everytime Brer Dog said something, Brer Rabbit jumped and twitched. All the animals noticed and started laughing at Brer Rabbit.

Brer Dog thought they were laughing at him. He started

growling and snapping. Brer Rabbit ducked under the chair. This made the animals laugh even more, and that made Brer Dog madder. He started howling, and Brer Rabbit shook like he'd caught a chill.

After a while Brer Dog quieted down, and Brer Rabbit eased out from under the chair. He got around among the other animals and began to do some politicking. "We ought to pass a law to make all the animals what eat with their teeth eat with their claws."

Brer Wolf, Brer Fox, and Brer Dog didn't like that idea one bit. So the law didn't pass. Next day Brer Rabbit started politicking again.

"Have you seen them teeth on Brer Dog? He got teeth like knives. We got to have a law to sew Brer Dog's mouth up. There's no telling what he might do with them teeth."

Now, that was a law Brer Wolf and Brer Fox could go along with. Brer Dog had chased them from can to can't on more than one occasion.

The law was passed. The day came for Brer Dog's mouth to be sewed up. Brer Lion was chairing the meeting, and he wanted to know who was going to sew up Brer Dog's mouth.

Brer Fox said, "The man what proposed the law ought to be the man to do the deed."

Brer Dog was laying over in the corner sharpening his teeth on a dinosaur bone. The animals looked at him and knew they weren't getting anywheres near him. They looked at Brer Rabbit.

He gave a little dry grin. "I'd sho' do it, but I ain't got a needle."

Brer Fox reached in the flap of his coat collar. "I got a big one right here, Brer Rabbit!"

Brer Rabbit gave another little grin. "Needle ain't no good without thread."

Brer Bear pulled a loose thread from his big ol' coat. "Here's some thread, Brer Rabbit."

Brer Rabbit said, "Thank you. I'd sho' appreciate it if you gentlemen would hold on to that needle and thread for me. I'm just sorry this matter didn't come up sooner 'cause this is the time of day I always take my walk."

And he tipped on out. The animals laughed at Brer Rabbit a long time about that one.

Brer Rabbit Advises Brer Lion

Brer Rabbit happened to see Brer Lion a week or so later. After they exchanged news about their families and what all, Brer Rabbit said, "Brer Lion, the times is changing."

"What you mean?"

"I'm moving back up in the hills, where it won't be so easy to find me."

"How come, Brer Rabbit? Something terrible must be happening for you to leave out of here."

Brer Rabbit nodded. "I've got to get away from Mr. Man."

Brer Lion laughed. "Mr. Man? You scared of Mr. Man? You got to be joking with me."

Brer Rabbit shook his head. "I'm not joking, Brer Lion."

Brer Lion roared. "I'm not scared of Mr. Man. I'll have Mr. Man for dinner if I come across him."

"Don't be too sure about that. Mr. Man got something

called a gun. It's like a stick, excepting he raises it up to his eye, points it at you, and goes *bang!* one time, and you get hit in the head. He go *bang!* a second time, and you get cripple in the leg."

Brer Lion laughed. "I'll take Mr. Man's gun, throw it away, and have Mr. Man for breakfast."

"Well, I tell you the truth. I'm scared."

Brer Lion said, "I can understand how you feel 'cause I'm scared of Miz Partridge."

Brer Rabbit couldn't believe his ears. "You scared of the wrong one, Brer Lion. Miz Partridge flies away if you wink at her. I'm not scared of Miz Partridge."

"Well, once I was walking along the road, and just as I went past some bushes, Miz Partridge flew up—*fud-d-d-d-d-e-c!* It liked to scared me to death."

Brer Rabbit shook his head. "Don't know about you, Brer Lion. You scared of what can't hurt you, and ain't scared of what can."

A few weeks went by, and Brer Rabbit was out walking one day when he heard a loud moaning sound. He went to investigate and found Brer Lion laying on the ground, moaning and groaning and crying. He had a hole in his head and three holes in his side.

Brer Rabbit looked at him. "Look like Miz Partridge done hurt you very bad, Brer Lion."

Brer Lion moaned and groaned and cried. "It wasn't Miz Partridge. It was Mr. Man with his gun."

Brer Rabbit nodded sadly. "That's what I tried to tell you, Brer Lion. Miz Partridge could *scare* you, but she couldn't hurt you. That's just what I was trying to tell you."

But it was too late for Brer Lion to learn that lesson.

Brer Rabbit's Money Mint

Brer Fox and Brer Rabbit were standing by the road talking about much of nothing. Brer Rabbit said that he was feeling between *My gracious!* and *Thank gracious!* Brer Fox say he know what he mean.

Brer Fox heard something rattling in Brer Rabbit's pocket. "Ain't that money I hear you rattling?"

Brer Rabbit shrugged. "Just small change." He took out a big handful of money. It was shining so bright that Brer Sun had to put on his sunglasses to keep from going blind.

"Where did you get it?"

"From where they make it at. The mint."

"Where's that at, Brer Rabbit?"

"In this place and that place. Over yonder and over here. You got to learn to keep your eyes open, Brer Fox."

"Learn me, Brer Rabbit! Please learn me!"

Brer Rabbit shook his head. "If I learn you, the next thing I know, word be spread all over the community, and I can't have that."

"I swear to you that I won't breathe a word to a soul."

Brer Rabbit thought about it for a minute, then shrugged. "All right. Ain't nothing to it. You just watch the road until you see a wagon come along. If it's the right kind of wagon, it's got two wheels in the front and two wheels in the back. And if you look real close, you'll notice that the wheels in the front are smaller than the ones in the back. Now, when you see that, what does it make you think of?"

Brer Fox thought and thought, but being as how he was kinna poor in the thinking department, he finally said, "I don't know, Brer Rabbit."

Brer Rabbit looked at Brer Fox like he was dumb as hog slop. "It's simple. After the wagon goes on for a ways, them big back wheels has got to catch up with them little front wheels. Common sense ought to tell you that."

Brer Fox nodded. "That's sho' the truth, ain't it?"

"Well, when the big back wheels catch up to the little front wheels, them wheels going to grind together. When that happens, all that brand-new money is going to fall out of the wagon."

Brer Fox clapped his hands. "And that's all there is to it?"

"That's it, Brer Fox. Next time you see a wagon going by, you call me if you don't want to follow along with it. I don't mind taking the money what drops down."

Well, along about then what do you think they heard? That's right! A wagon!

"I'll take this wagon, Brer Rabbit."

Brer Rabbit shrugged. "Help yourself. I got to be getting on home anyway."

Brer Rabbit left, but he circled back to watch Brer Fox. Sure enough, when the wagon passed, Brer Fox started galloping alongside, waiting for the back wheels to catch up to the front wheels. Some folks say he's galloping still.

Brer Rabbit Makes a Deal with Mr. Man

Mr. Man was going around his farm one day when he noticed that a pig was missing. Day after that a duck was missing. The day after that a chicken was gone.

Mr. Man might not have been the smartest person on the top side of the earth, but he knew something was going on. He made a trap and put a chicken in it.

First thing next morning Mr. Man went to see about his trap. In it was Brer Fox and a whole bunch of chicken feathers.

Brer Fox gave one of his little dry grins. "You probably won't believe this, but I was passing by on my way home last night and heard a chicken hollering and fluttering. I came in to see what was the matter. As I came in, the chicken went out and shut the door, leaving all these feathers behind."

Mr. Man gave a little grunt. "If that chicken hollered right now, I bet she would scare you."

"How so?"

" 'Cause she so close to you."

Mr. Man got a rope, tied Brer Fox tightly, and then took him home and hung him on a nail on the wall. "Keep your eye on him until I get back," Mr. Man told his wife.

Mr. Man's wife was shelling peas.

"That's a lot of peas you got to shell," Brer Fox offered.

"You said a mouthful."

Brer Fox had been tricked by Brer Rabbit so many times that he was bound to learn something about scheming. "If you'll untie me and take me down from here, I'll shell them peas for you, and you can be fixing the rest of the dinner. And when I'm done, you can tie me again and hang me back on the wall."

The woman shook her head. Brer Fox kept on talking and he talked sweet and he talked low and he talked so much stuff that Mr. Man's wife decided that he couldn't be as bad as her husband thought. So she took him down and untied him.

Brer Fox started shelling peas. The woman stirred her stew. Brer Fox kept one eye on her. She kept one eye on him. They kept eyeing each other until suddenly Brer Fox made a break for the door. The woman was just a little quicker. She slammed the door shut, grabbed a stick, and started chasing Brer Fox around the room. Brer Fox dashed up the chimney, and as he did so, he turned over the pot of stew, which put out the fire and scalded the woman's foot. She screamed, and Brer Fox got away from there.

When Mr. Man came home, he wasn't none too happy when he found out what had happened. He yelled at the woman, and she started crying. He kept on yelling until she got mad: "What you mean calling me an airhead for letting Brer Fox get away? You the one got more holes in your head than Swiss cheese. If you'd had any sense, you would've killed that fox when you had him. Now you want to blame it on me, and I ain't taking the heavy for this one!"

Mr. Man had to admit that his wife had a point. He apologized and took a walk in the field. He was feeling mighty bad about everything.

Brer Rabbit was taking his evening stroll when he saw Mr. Man sitting on a fence like he didn't have a friend in the world. Brer Rabbit went over and asked what was the matter. Mr. Man told him. Brer Rabbit chuckled.

"Looks like Brer Fox done learned a thing or two from me. If I ain't careful, he gon' start thinking he's smart as me." He thought for a minute. "Mr. Man? How much will you give me if I make Brer Fox sorry for what he done to you and your wife?"

"Brer Rabbit, you can eat all the peanuts and all the cabbage in my garden that you want."

"And you won't set your dogs on me?"

"No, sir."

Brer Rabbit stuck out his hand, and they shook. "We got a deal."

He thought for a while longer. "I'm going to need some chicken gizzards."

Mr. Man got them and came back. "Anything else?"

"This is just fine. I be back in the morning to start in on your peanut patch."

Brer Rabbit put the chicken gizzards in a sack and started toward Brer Fox's house. He hadn't gone far when he came upon him. They exchanged all the news about their kin, but while they were doing this, Brer Fox was sniffing the air.

"Brer Rabbit, I believe I smell chicken gizzards."

"I reckon that's so, Brer Fox. I got some right here in this sack."

Brer Fox started licking his lips. "How many you got?"

"Somewhere between seven and eleven."

"What you planning on doing with 'em?"

"I'm going to give 'em to the man who helps me with my hay."

"Show me the hay!" Brer Fox exclaimed, jumping up in the air. "Show me the hay! I'll carry that hay anywheres you want."

So Brer Rabbit and Brer Fox went over to the hayfield. Brer Rabbit started loading hay on Brer Fox's back until he looked like a haystack with fox feet.

They started up the hill. Brer Rabbit took out his flint and steel and struck it on the hay.

"What's that noise?" Brer Fox wanted to know.

"Cricket."

The hay started to crackle and blaze.

"What's *that* noise?"

"Grasshopper singing."

The hay started to burn good.

"I smell smoke."

"Somebody's burning new ground."

"I sho' do feel hot."

"You working hard."

Before long the hay burned down on Brer Fox. He yelled and scooted out from under. He jumped; he twisted; he turned; he rolled, but that fire was just burning him. He ran to the creek and jumped in. When he came out, the hair was burned off his back and his hide was full of blisters.

That's just what he gets for not being patient and waiting until he could get away clean without scalding Mr. Man's wife.

Brer Rabbit Doctors Brer Fox's Burns

Brer Rabbit decided he wasn't done with Brer Fox. He got a string of red pepper, stewed it down with some hog fat and mutton suet. He picked out the pepper and let the fat and suet get cold and thick, spread it on a piece of rag, and set off for Brer Fox's house.

When he got close, he saw Brer Fox sitting on the porch looking miserable. Brer Rabbit started yelling, "Ointment! Salve for burns and blisters!" He walked past Brer Fox's house like he didn't see him.

"Brer Rabbit!" called Brer Fox.

Brer Rabbit kept walking.

"BRER RABBIT!"

Brer Rabbit turned around and looked at Brer Fox. Then he went on down the road like he hadn't seen him.

Brer Fox caught up with him. "Didn't you hear me calling you?"

Brer Rabbit whirled around, and he was angry! "What you want and make it quick! I ain't got time for the likes of you!"

Brer Fox was confused. "What you mad at me about?"

"What am I mad at you about? My hay, that's what! You said you was going to carry it up the hill for me."

"But, Brer Rabbit! You saw with your own eyes why I couldn't! The sun set the hay on fire. I was lucky to escape with my life."

Brer Rabbit thought for a minute. "Well, you sho' got the marks on your back. I thought you were playing one of your tricks on me. To tell the truth, my feelings were hurt."

Brer Fox was in so much misery, he didn't have time to be worrying about hurt feelings. "I heard you hollering that you got some salve for burns and blisters."

Brer Rabbit pulled out the rag. "This'll do the trick. Get your wife to spread it all over you as soon as you can."

Brer Fox took it and went home. Brer Rabbit hid in the bushes to watch. Hardly a minute passed before Brer Fox gave out with a scream that curdled all the milk for miles around. He bust through the door and in seven jumps was in the creek, and the creek was almost a mile away.

Brer Rabbit followed, and it was all he could do to keep from busting out laughing.

Brer Fox looked like a dolphin the way he was jumping up and down in the water.

"My goodness, Brer Fox! Is that a new style of fishing you doing?"

"Brer Rabbit! You done ruined me! That stuff you gave me was poison!"

Brer Rabbit looked astonished. "Did I gave you the wrong salve?" He looked in his pouch. "I'm so sorry, Brer Fox! Instead of giving you the n'yam-n'yam plaster, I gave you the n'yip-n'yip plaster. I must be losing all my seventy senses."

And he fell back in the weeds and laughed until he was sick.

Brer Fox Sets a Fire

Brer Fox decided he'd better let Brer Rabbit alone for a while. He was still mad, though, and if he couldn't get the best of Brer Rabbit, he'd do something to one of the other animals.

As he was walking down the road thinking these very thoughts, who should he see but Brer Turtle. If he could whup anybody, it had to be Brer Turtle.

"How you today, Brer Turtle?"

"Slow, Brer Fox. Mighty slow. Day in and day out I'm slow, and looks like I'm getting slower. How you today?"

"Fine, just fine. Say, Brer Turtle? Your eyes are red. How come?"

"It's on account of all the trouble I see. Trouble come and pile up on trouble."

Brer Fox laughed. "Listen here, Brer Turtle. You don't know what trouble is! If you want to see some trouble, you ought to come with me. I'll show you trouble!"

"Well, if you can show me worst trouble, I'm the one wants to glimpse it."

Brer Fox asked him if he had ever seen Ol' Boy. Brer Turtle said he hadn't, but he'd heard of him. Brer Fox said that Ol' Boy was the kind of trouble he was talking about.

"Let me see him," said Brer Turtle. "It'll make me feel better to see worse trouble than what I got."

"All right! Tell you what you do. Go lay down in that sagebrush field yonder, and before long you'll catch a glimpse of Ol' Boy."

When Brer Turtle had been sitting in the middle of the field for a while, Brer Fox set the field on fire. Fire was blazing up everywhere, and right there in the middle of it was po' Brer Turtle.

He started moving fast as he could to get away, and you know about how fast that was. But he was doing his best, and he stumbled across Brer Rabbit, who was asleep behind a log. Brer Rabbit woke up, looked around, and knew that they were going to be shaking hands with Ol' Boy if he didn't do something.

"What we gon' do, Brer Rabbit?"

"There's a big hollow stump right over here. Come on!"

Brer Rabbit carried him over to the stump, and they crawled in. Brer Rabbit went back to sleep so's he could finish his nap.

When the fire died down, Brer Turtle stuck his head up out of the stump. Brer Fox was at the edge of the field, craning his neck trying to see through the smoke. Brer

Rabbit woke up, saw Brer Fox, and hollered out like he was Brer Turtle: "Brer Fox! Oh, Brer Fox! Come here! Quick! I done caught Brer Rabbit!"

Without thinking Brer Fox started running across the field. It was still hot from the fire, and his feet were burnt almost to ashes. He hopped and screamed and jumped and ouched and rolled on the ground, which only made it worse. Finally he managed to get back on cool ground and started making his way home, hopping first on one foot and then the other. Brer Rabbit and Brer Turtle followed him all the way, laughing every step he took.

Brer Rabbit Builds a Tower

Well, the animals decided something had to be done about Brer Rabbit. They talked it over among themselves and agreed that from then on Brer Rabbit couldn't drink out of the same creek with them, walk the same road, or go washing in the same wash hole.

When Brer Rabbit saw the animals holding secret meetings, he knew that something was up, so he reinforced his house, put in some Plexiglass windows, new locks on the doors, and started building a steeple on top.

Folks wondered what he was up to, and some thought he was building his own church.

Brer Rabbit didn't pay 'em no mind. He hammered; he nailed; he knocked; he lammed! Folks hollered at him, but he wouldn't look up. He just worked from sunup to moonrise.

When he finished, he took a deep breath, wiped his brow, and went in the house. He got a long piece of thick rope and told his wife, "Put a kettle of water on the fire and stay close by. I'm going up to the steeple, and everything you hear me tell you not to do, you do!"

He went back up to his steeple, sat down in his rocking chair, and looked out over the landscape.

Wasn't long before the animals came to see what he was going to do next. He didn't do a thing except smoke his cigar and rock in his rocking chair.

Brer Turtle came along. "Hey, Brer Rabbit!" he hollered up. "What you doing way up in the elements like that?"

"Resting myself. Why don't you come up and visit, Brer Turtle?"

Brer Turtle shook his head. "Too far in the air for me. Why don't you come down? I'm afraid to shake hands with you that far up in the elements."

"Not so, Brer Turtle. Not so. Come on up." Brer Rabbit let down the rope. "Just grab on, and up you'll come, *linktum sinktum blinktum boo!*"

So Brer Turtle grabbed the rope in his mouth, and Brer Rabbit pulled him up. That was a sight to see, his little tail sticking out, his legs wiggling, and him spinning around in the air half-scared to death.

But he made it safe and sound, and Brer Rabbit offered him some lunch. When the other animals saw Brer Turtle and Brer Rabbit up there chewing and smacking their lips, they wanted to come up.

"Hey, Brer Rabbit!" called out Brer Wolf. "How you doing?"

"Not too good," responded Brer Rabbit. "But I thank the Lord that I'm still able to chew my food. Why don't you come on up, Brer Wolf?"

"Don't mind if I do."

Brer Rabbit let down the rope. Brer Wolf caught hold, and Brer Rabbit started to haul him up.

"Stir 'round, ol' woman, and set the table. But before you do that, get the kettle to make the coffee."

Brer Wolf wondered what Brer Rabbit was talking about.

Brer Rabbit pulled on the rope until Brer Wolf was just opposite the upstairs bedroom window of the house.

"Watch out there, ol' woman! Don't spill all that hot

boiling water on Brer Wolf!"

Brer Wolf didn't hear another word because Miz Rabbit threw the kettle of boiling water out the window on him. Brer Wolf hollered and fell to the ground—*ka-boom*!

Brer Rabbit looked down from the steeple and apologized, but all the apologies in the world wasn't going to make hair grow back on Brer Wolf.

Brer Rabbit Saves Brer Wolf—Maybe

Brer Wolf had to go away to get himself a wolf wig, so Brer Rabbit decided it was safe to come out of his steeple. He was so happy to be out that he got dressed up and strutted down the road like he'd just discovered where the lights go when you turn 'em out.

He hadn't gone far when he heard somebody hollering: "Oh, Lordy! Won't somebody help me!"

Brer Rabbit turned this way and that trying to figure out where it was coming from.

"Help! Please help me, somebody!"

"Where you at?" Brer Rabbit called back.

"Help! Please help me! I'm down here in the gully underneath a great big rock!"

Brer Rabbit ran down to the gully, and there, under a great big rock, was none other than Brer Wolf! The sweat was pouring off him, and he looked pitiful. Not liking to see somebody in trouble that he hadn't put 'em in, Brer Rabbit felt sorry for Brer Wolf.

It took him a while, but he finally managed to roll the

rock off. Brer Wolf was hurt more in his feelings than any place else, and it occurred to him that he probably wouldn't ever have a better chance to grab Brer Rabbit. So that was what he did!

Brer Rabbit kicked and squealed, and the more he kicked, the tighter Brer Wolf squeezed his neck.

"Is this the way you thank a body for saving your life?"

Brer Wolf grinned. "I'll thank you, and then I'll make fresh meat out of you."

"If you talk that way, I'll never do you another good turn as long as I live."

Brer Wolf grinned some more. "You spoke truth that time, Brer Rabbit. You won't do me another good turn until you're dead."

Brer Rabbit shook his head. "There's a law in this community what say you can't kill folks who've done you a favor."

"I ain't never heard of no such law," Brer Wolf responded, confused now.

"Well, let's go see Brer Turtle. He know the law."

So off they went to Brer Turtle's house, where Brer Wolf explained his side, and Brer Rabbit explained his.

Brer Turtle put on his glasses and cleared his throat. "This is a mixed-up case. Ain't no doubt about that. Before I can see which side the law come down on, I got to see the place where the incident took place."

They carried Brer Turtle down to the gully and showed him where Brer Wolf had been trapped under the rock. Brer Turtle walked around and poked at the spot with his cane. Then he shook his head. "I hate to put y'all to so much trouble, but I have to see how the rock was lying on Brer Wolf."

Brer Wolf lay down, and Brer Rabbit rolled the rock back on top of him. Brer Turtle walked around and around. He made some marks on the ground, stared at them, and walked around some more.

"Say, Brer Turtle. This rock is getting kinna heavy."

Brer Turtle made some more marks on the ground and did some more walking around, deep in thought.

"Brer Turtle! This rock is squeezing the breath out of me."

Brer Turtle took his glasses off and cleared his throat. "I have reached my decision. Brer Rabbit! You were in the wrong. You didn't have no business coming along and bothering Brer Wolf when he wasn't bothering you. He was minding his business, and you ought to have been minding yours."

Brer Rabbit looked ashamed.

"When you were going down the road yonder, I know you were going somewhere. If you were going somewhere, you should've gone on. Brer Wolf wasn't going nowhere then, and he ain't going nowhere now. You found him under that rock, and under that rock you should've left him."

Brer Rabbit thanked Brer Turtle for his legal wisdom. They gave each other high fives and went on to town talking about what a smart man Brer Turtle was.

Mammy-Bammy Big-Money Takes Care of Brer Wolf

Aunt Mammy-Bammy Big-Money got sick and tired of Brer Wolf taking up space in the world. And when Mammy-Bammy Big-Money said your time had come, you best make your reservation with the gravedigger.

Mammy-Bammy Big-Money was the witch rabbit, and she knew everything that was going on. She sent word to Brer Rabbit that she wanted to see him.

She lived way off in a deep, dark swamp between Lost Forty and the outskirts of Hell, and to get there, you had to ride some, slide some; jump some, hump some; hop some, flop some; walk some, balk some; creep some, sleep some; fly some, cry some; follow some, holler some; wade some, spade some; and if you weren't careful, you still might miss the turnoff. Brer Rabbit got there, but he was plumb wore out when he did.

He and Mammy-Bammy Big-Money talked for a long while about how they were going to rid the world of Brer Wolf. They finally got their plan all fixed up, and Brer Rabbit went on back.

A few days later Brer Rabbit ran into Brer Wolf's house all out of breath. "Brer Wolf! Brer Wolf! I just came from the river, and Mammy-Bammy Big-Money is lying there dead! Let's go eat her up!"

"You lying, Brer Rabbit."

"I ain't telling no tale, Brer Wolf. Come on! Let's go!"

"You sure she's dead?"

"Brer Wolf, she dead, I'm telling you! A body can't get no more dead. Let's go!"

They got all the other animals together, and by the time they got down to the river, so many folks were there, you would've thought it was a rock concert. Everybody could see with their own eyes that Brer Rabbit hadn't lied. Mammy-Bammy Big-Money was deader than death. Brer Wolf jumped up in the air, clicked his heels, and let out a holler!

The problem now was how to divide up her carcass. He asked Brer Mink, Brer Coon, Brer Possum, Brer Turtle, and Brer Rabbit what part they wanted. They all agreed that since he was the biggest and had the biggest appetite, he should get first choice.

Brer Wolf nodded, pleased. He turned to Brer Coon and said, "You and me been friends since Ol' Boy was in diapers. How much of this meat you think an old feeble man like me ought to take?"

"Why don't you take one of the forequarters?"

Brer Wolf was astonished. "Have mercy, Brer Coon! I thought you was my friend. From the way you talk, I can tell you ain't got no feeling for me. What you say leaves me feeling on the lonely side. Brer Mink! You and me been knowing each other since before Santa Claus had a beard. How much of this meat you think ought to be my share?"

"I reckon you should get one of the forequarters and a big chunk off the bulge of the neck."

"Get away from here, Brer Mink! I don't want to know you if you talk like that. Brer Possum! I been knowing you since before rainwater found out it could turn to snowflakes. Look at me, look at my family, and then tell me how much of this meat should be my share."

Brer Possum thought for a minute. "Take half, Brer Wolf! Take half!"

Brer Wolf shook his head in dismay. "And I thought you knew something about friendship. I can't believe what I'm hearing."

Brer Wolf asked Brer Turtle, who told him to take everything except one of the hindquarters. Brer Wolf shook his head. "I never did think that folks who said they were my friends would want to starve me like this."

Then Brer Wolf asked Brer Rabbit for his opinion.

Brer Rabbit stood up. "Gentlemen, take a look at Brer Wolf's family. Just by looking at 'em you can tell that they're hungry, and you know Brer Wolf is monstrously hungry. Takes a lot of meat to keep a family of wolves going. So I'm going to put it to you straight: Brer Wolf should have first chance at Big-Money. I say we tie him on and let him eat as much as he wants, and we can have whatever's left."

Brer Wolf laughed. "I knowed you was my partner, Brer Rabbit! You my honey partner!"

They tied Brer Wolf on to Mammy-Bammy Big-Money.

Brer Wolf bit her on the neck. Mammy-Bammy Big-Money twitched and jumped up. Brer Wolf hollered, "Come here, somebody! Get me off here! She ain't dead!"

Brer Rabbit yelled back, "Never mind that, Brer Wolf! She dead! Sho' 'nuf. She dead! Bite her again!"

Brer Wolf bent over and bit her again, and Mammy-Bammy Big-Money started running. Brer Wolf was hollering like the world had caught fire: "Help! Get me off here! Help, somebody! Untie me, Brer Rabbit! Untie me!"

Brer Rabbit shouted back, "She dead, Brer Wolf! She dead! Nail her, Brer Wolf! Bite her! Gnaw her!"

Brer Wolf went back to biting, and Mammy-Bammy Big-Money kept running along the riverbank until she came to the deepest part of the river. She picked up speed, leaped, and landed—*cumberjoom!*—right smack in the middle of the river. She turned over on her back and stayed that way until Brer Wolf was drowned dead.

Brer Rabbit and the Gizzard Eater

Among the animals nobody could out-party Brer Rabbit. He knew all the dances from the waltz to the tango to the twist, and way I hear it, he invented discoing and break-dancing. But don't quote me on that.

One time, however, Brer Rabbit partied too much, 'cause a big rainstorm came up, and when Brer Rabbit put out for home, the streams had become creeks and the creeks rivers and the rivers—well, if I told you what the rivers had become, you'd accuse me of having told truth goodbye.

Brer Rabbit had to backtrack and go 'round this way and that before he got as far as the creek close to his house. Many times he'd walked across that creek on a log, but the log had washed away. The creek was big and wide now, and it made him feel like he'd been lost so long that his family had forgotten him. And it was the wettest wet water Brer Rabbit had ever seen.

Brer Rabbit thought if he could holler loud enough, maybe somebody would come fetch him a boat. So he set in to hollering: "HEY, SOMEBODY! HEEEEEY! HEEEEYOOOOOOO!"

All that racket woke up Brer Alligator, who was sleeping at the bottom of the creek. *Who's that trying to holler the bottom out of the creek?* he wondered.

He rose to the top like he wasn't nothing more than a cork. He looked around with his two eyes like two bullets floating on the water. Then he saw Brer Rabbit.

"What's happening, Brer Rabbit? How's your daughter?"

Brer Alligator had had eyes for Brer Rabbit's daughter for a long time.

"She ain't doing too well, Brer 'Gator. When I left home, her head was all swole up. Some of the neighbor's children been flinging rocks at her, and one hit right smack on top of her head, and I had to run for the doctor."

Brer Alligator shook his head. "Don't know what the world's coming to, Brer Rabbit. Pretty soon won't be no peace nowhere except in my bed at the bottom of the creek."

"Ain't that the truth! And no sooner than I go for the doctor than this storm come along, and all the streams rose up like they mad at somebody. I'm over here, and my daughter is over there, waiting for me to bring the medicine the doctor gave me. I would try to swim across, but I'm afraid that these pills in my pocket might melt. And I might get poisoned then, since the doctor say the pills supposed to go *in* you, not *on* you."

Brer Alligator floated on top of the water like he didn't weigh more than a postage stamp, and he looked like he was about to cry. "Well, Brer Rabbit, if there ever was a rover, you the one. Up you come and off you go, and there ain't no more keeping up with you than if you had wings. If you think you can stay put in one place long enough, I'll take you across the creek."

Brer Rabbit rubbed his chin. "Brer 'Gator, how deep is that water?"

"Well, if I stood up straight in the water, there'd be enough room beneath my tail for my wife and my children to stand up straight and still not touch bottom."

Brer Rabbit moved back from the edge and looked like he was going to faint. "That makes me feel farther from home than them what's done lost for good! How in the world you going to get me across this slippery water?"

"Take you across on my back, but don't go around telling folks that I decided to be a water horse."

"I wouldn't say nothing to nobody about it, Brer 'Gator, but listen here. I heard that your tail is mighty limber. I heard you can knock a chip from the back of your head with the tip end of your tail and not even be half-trying."

"That's true, Brer Rabbit, but don't hold it against me. That's the way Ol' Maker put me together, so that's the way I be."

Brer Rabbit thought for a while and finally said, "Well, that sounds like it's somewhere in the neighborhood of the truth, so I reckon I'll let you carry me across."

Brer Alligator floated over to the bank, smiling as he came. His teeth looked like they more properly belonged in a sawmill than in a creature's mouth, and Brer Rabbit started shaking like he'd caught a chill.

"Brer 'Gator, your back is mighty rough. How am I going to ride on it?"

"The roughness will help you hold on. You can fit your feet on the bumps and be as comfortable as if you were at home in your rocking chair."

Brer Rabbit got on and immediately wished he was off, but Brer Alligator slid off through the water like he was greased.

Brer Rabbit was scared, especially when he noticed that Brer Alligator wasn't headed for the landing place on the other side of the creek. "Brer 'Gator? If I ain't mistaken, you ain't heading for the landing."

Brer Alligator grinned a toothy grin. "You sho' got good eyes, Brer Rabbit. I been waiting a long, long time for

you. You probably done forgot that day when you said you was going to show me Ol' Man Trouble. Well, you not only showed him to me; you had m e shake hands with him when you set that dry grass on fire and near 'bout burned me up. That's the reason my back is so rough now and my hide is so tough. Well, I've been waiting for you since then, and here you are."

Brer Alligator laughed. Brer Rabbit didn't see what was funny. He just sat there, shaking and quivering. Finally he asked in a weak voice, "What you gon' do with me, Brer 'Gator?"

"Well, ever since that fire I ain't been myself. I went to the doctor, and he say my condition is getting worse. All the smoke from that fire done something to my insides, and there's only one thing can cure me."

"What's that?" Brer Rabbit wasn't sure he wanted to know.

"Rabbit gizzard," Brer Alligator said, grinning a toothy grin.

Brer Rabbit laughed then. "Well, this is both our lucky day, Brer 'Gator."

"I know it's mine, but how is it yours?"

"Well, I've been feeling kinna po'ly myself. The doctor told me my problem was that I had a double gizzard, and one of my gizzards had to be took out, but he don't know how to do it. Say it's a job for the gizzard eater. Well, I asked him where I could find the gizzard eater. He say he don't know, but when I meet up with him, I'd know it."

Brer Alligator kept slipping through the water, but he don't say nothing.

"What I'm telling you is the fatal truth," Brer Rabbit continued. "Doctor told me that the worst thing a man with a double gizzard could do would be to cross the water with that double gizzard in him. If that gizzard smell water, I'll swell up so bad my skin couldn't hold me. So that's why last night, when I came to cross this creek, I took out my double gizzard and hid it in a hollow hickory log. Now, since you obviously a gizzard eater, you can help me get shed of the thing. If you in the mood, I'll take you right to the stump and show you where I hid it. Or, if you want to be lonesome about it, I'll let you go by yourself, and I'll stay here."

"Where you say you'll stay?"

"Anywhere you want me to, Brer 'Gator. I don't care where I stay just so long as I get rid of that double gizzard. It probably be best if you go by yourself, because as much trouble as that double gizzard gives me, I feel kind of sentimental about it. If I see you gobble it up, I just might start boohooing, and that wouldn't be no good for your digestion. If you go by yourself, just rap on the stump and say 'If you are ready, *I'm* ready and a little more so.' The gizzard won't give you no trouble then. I hid it right there in them woods yonder."

Brer Alligator had about as much sense as the man who tried to climb a fence after somebody knocked it down. He went on through the water to the landing, and Brer Rabbit took a big leap onto solid ground. He turned around and sang out:

> *You po' ol' 'gator, if you knew A from izzard,*
> *You'd know mighty well that I'd keep my gizzard.*

And with that he was gone!

Why Dogs Are Always Sniffing

Before Brer Lion was Brer Lion, he was King Lion, and he was king of all the animals. There wasn't much to kinging back in them days. All he did was sit on his throne chair every day and hold his crown on his head.

He had been sitting there holding his crown on his head for seventy-eleven years and one day decided to go out and have some fun, like them he'd been kinging it over. He called his advisors together and told them what he had in mind and wanted to know what he should do.

They talked it over and decided that the best thing would be for the king to go fishing. He liked that idea. So all the folks what worked in the palace ran around getting together everything the king would need—pole and line and hooks and bait, a chair to sit on, and a lot of fish. It wouldn't do for the king to go fishing and not catch nothing.

When the king was ready to go, Brer Rabbit started giggling.

"What's so funny?" the king wanted to know.

"Ain't none of my business, but seems to me that you done forgot something."

"What's that, Brer Rabbit?"

"Who gon' do the kinging while you fishing?"

The king threw up his hands and shook his head. "I don't know what's the matter with me. How could I forget something like that?"

Brer Rabbit shrugged. "It probably don't matter 'cause don't nothing ever happen nohow."

"That ain't the point," the king insisted. "Here I was about to go out and have some fun and leave everything to look after itself. I tell you the truth, there ain't no fun in being king. Your time ain't your own, and everytime you turn around, you hurt your knee running into some bylaw. Somebody got to be king today." The king sat down and thought for a long time. Finally he said, "Brer Rabbit, what about you? I'll pay you a dollar, and you can sit in my throne chair and hold the crown on your head."

That sounded all right to Brer Rabbit. The ol' woman had been on him about buying her some flowers so she would know he loved her. The dollar would come in handy.

The king went fishing, and Brer Rabbit sat down on the throne chair. Of course, he wasn't about to sit there and hold a crown on his head all day. He sent one of the servants for some string and tied the crown on his head and made a little bow under his chin.

Wasn't long before he heard a lot of howling and growling and whining outside.

"What's going on?" Brer Rabbit wanted to know.

One of the advisors said, "Well, if the king was here, he wouldn't pay no attention to all that noise. The king would wait until somebody came and told somebody what the racket was about, and that somebody would tell somebody else, and maybe, about dinnertime, the word might or might not get to the king."

Brer Rabbit said, "If the king would get up and look out the window, he'd know what the racket was."

"That ain't kinging," said the advisor.

Brer Rabbit said, "Oh," and sat back down in the throne chair and went to sleep. Long about dinnertime one of the advisors came in and said Brer Dog had to see the king. Brer Rabbit rubbed the sleep out of his eyes and said to show Brer Dog in.

Brer Dog came in, and he was a pathetic-looking thing.

He looked so hungry that you could count all the ribs in his body. He was so skinny, he didn't even cast a shadow. He had his head down and was shivering all over like he was cold.

Brer Rabbit looked at him closely to see if he knew this dog. Sure enough, it was the very same dog that had been chasing him all over the countryside for more years than Brer Rabbit could count.

Brer Dog stood there with his head hanging down and his tail between his legs. He didn't look like he had the strength to jump on a broken-down truck full of raw hamburger meat.

"What's your business with the king?" one of the advisors asked.

Brer Dog started moaning. "I'm having the worse time anybody on the top side of the world has ever had. We used to get meat. Now we get bones and not too many of them. We used to be able to run all through the countryside. Now Mr. Man wants to lock us up in the house and call us Fido or Spot. Used to be a time when a dog was respected. But it ain't like that no more. Anything the king could do to help us sho' would be appreciated."

Brer Rabbit studied over the situation. Finally he turned to one of his advisors and asked if there was any turpentine around. The advisor said he thought they could find some.

"Mix together a pound of red peppers with the turpentine and bring it to me."

The advisor had it done, and it was brought to Brer Rabbit. He grabbed Brer Dog and rubbed the turpentine and red peppers all over his body. Brer Dog howled and ran out of the palace as fast as he could.

Day followed day just the same way they do now, and Brer Dog didn't come back home. His kinfolk got worried. They waited a few weeks more, and still no sign of Brer Dog. So they went to see the king to ask him if he knew where Brer Dog was.

Naturally they didn't get to see the king, but they saw one of the advisors, who told them that Brer Dog had been there and had seen the king and that the king had given him what he'd come after.

The dogs looked at each other. "He ain't come back home," said one of 'em.

"You'd better hunt him up, then, and find out what he did with what the king gave him."

"But how we going to know him when we find him?" the dogs wanted to know.

"You'll be able to tell him by the smell of the turpentine and red pepper the king put on him to kill his fleas and cure his bites."

Well, from that day to this the dogs have been hunting for Brer Dog. They been smelling along the ground; they smell the trees and the stumps and the bushes, and when they see a dog they don't know, they smell him. Sometimes they smell a bush or a stump or something and start growling and scratching the ground, practicing what they're going to do when they catch up to Brer Dog. So when you see a dog come sniffing along, you let him go on his way 'cause one of these days I believe they just might catch up to Brer Dog.

Being Fashionable Ain't Always Healthy

One Septerarry an awful storm hit the part of the country where the animals lived. The animals were afraid they were going to be blown to the other side of the world if they stayed on the top side. They managed to come through the storm all right, but an animal that lived way far away didn't make out too good.

That was ol' Craney Crow. Folks call 'em herons now, but back in them times he had a name what somebody could say, and it sounded like English.

The storm was even worse down in Craney Crow's country. That wind got a hold of Craney Crow and turned him around and around in the air. When it set him down, he was up in the animals' part of the world.

Craney Crow didn't know where he was. He wasn't even too sure that he was. He'd been whirled around so much that he leaned against a tree like a drunk man for an hour or so before he thought about trying to walk.

When he was feeling more like himself, he looked around to see where he was. He couldn't see a thing because it was the middle of the night. All he knew was that he was a long way from home. There was water halfway up his legs, and that felt familiar 'cause Craney Crow had always lived where he could wade in the water.

What Craney Crow didn't know was that the wind had set him down in the Long Cane Swamp. After a while the Sun started to rise and shine his lamp into the Swamp, and Craney Crow could see. But seeing didn't tell him any more than not seeing had.

The Swamp knew somebody was in it who didn't be-long there, and it was disturbed. But the Sun was coming up, so the Swamp went to sleep, 'cause that's when it slept. The Swamp had the worst sleep that day it had ever had, before or since. It had nothing but bad dreams and daymares.

After a while the Sun stood right above the Swamp. Even it knew something was wrong. He wanted to see in and shone as much of his light into the dark Swamp as he could but couldn't see nothing. Bright as the lamp of the Sun is, it can't light up the Swamp. So it went on its way to the other side of the world.

While the Sun was arching over the Swamp trying to find out what the trouble was, Craney Crow was wading around in the water, looking for a frog or a fish to take the edge off his appetite. But there wasn't a frog or fish to be seen. The Swamp had gone to sleep.

Ol' Craney Crow walked around, his eyes as wide open as a fresh-dug grave. He'd never seen anything like the Swamp in his life. He was used to grass and water. There was nothing here but vines, and reeds, and trees with moss on them that made 'em look like Gransir Graybeard. The vines and creepers looked like they were reaching out for him.

He walked around like the ground was hot. He didn't know how in the world he was going to make his home in such a strange place.

Toward evening Craney Crow walked out of the water onto the muddy bank. The Swamp yawned and stretched itself. Brer Mud Turtle opened his eyes and sneezed so hard that he rolled off the bank into the water—*kersplash!* Craney Crow jumped back and almost stepped on Brer Billy Black Snake. That scared him so much that he jumped back again and near 'bout landed on a frog, which is what he'd been looking for all day.

Craney Crow was so scared by all the creatures coming to life that he didn't even think about eating the frog. Jack-o-lanterns were flying around, their lights blinking on and off like they were looking for him. The frogs hollered at him, *"What're you doing here? What're you doing here?"* The coon ran by and laughed at him. Mr. Billy Gray Fox peeped out of a clump of bushes and barked at him. Mr. Mink peeped his green eyes at him, and the whipperwill scolded him.

After a while all the creatures left him alone and went about their business. Ol' Craney Crow started moving around again. He noticed that the birds that flew around in the daytime were going to bed without their heads. He looked into a lot of bushes, and sure enough, all the day birds had all gone to sleep without their heads.

Craney Crow had never seen such a thing. That must be the custom of the day birds in this part of the country. Craney Crow wanted so much to be a part of this new community the wind had placed him down in. But how could he if he went to sleep with his head on? Of course, if Craney Crow had looked real close, or if his eyes had been more accustomed to the night, he would've seen that the birds had simply tucked their heads under their wings. But Craney Crow didn't see that.

It was long past Craney Crow's bedtime. He looked around and saw Brer Pop-Eye staring at him. That was what Brer Rabbit called himself when he went down to the low country.

"How do, Mr. Craney Crow," said Brer Pop-Eye.

"How do, Brer Pop-Eye. You might be just the man I'm looking for. Would you be good enough to tell me something?"

"If I know it, I'll tell it to you."

"I'd sho' appreciate it. What I want to know is this: How do all the flying birds take their heads off when they go to bed? I just can't figure out how they do it."

"I ain't surprised, Mr. Craney Crow. You a stranger in these parts. The mosquitoes in this Swamp are so awful that the only way the birds can get some sleep is to take their heads off and put 'em someplace where the mosquitoes can't get them."

"But how in the world do they do it, Brer Pop-Eye?"

Brer Pop-Eye laughed. "They don't do it by themselves. No, indeed! They hired someone to do it for them."

"Where can I find him? I sho' would like to get some sleep."

"You stay right here. He be around soon. He's probably checking to make sure he ain't missed nobody."

Mr. Craney Crow thought for a moment. "Tell me this. How do they get their heads back on?"

Brer Pop-Eye shook his head. "Can't tell you. I'm a night person myself. About the time they be getting their heads back on is about the time I go to sleep. But if you want me to, I'll hunt up the man in charge of taking their heads off."

Ol' Craney Crow thanked him. Brer Pop-Eye took off and came back in a little while with Brer Wolf. Brer Wolf's tongue was hanging out of his mouth and dripping so much wet it made a puddle at his feet.

"This is Dock Wolf. Dock, this is Mr. Craney Crow."

Craney Crow told Dock Wolf how much he wanted to go to sleep like the other birds so maybe they'd be friends with him in the morning.

Dock Wolf put his thumb in his vest holes and looked like a sho' 'nuf doctor. "I don't know as I can help you,

Mr. Craney Crow. To tell the truth, I ain't never seen a creature with such a long neck as yours."

He felt Craney Crow's neck tenderly, running his hands up and down it. "Hold your head lower, Mr. Craney Crow." Mr. Craney Crow did and—*snap*—that was the last of Mr. Craney Crow. Brer Wolf slung him over his back and trotted on home. But that was after him and Brer Rabbit gave each other high fives.

Brer Rabbit decided it was time for him to get on home too. It took longer than it should have because he couldn't walk for laughing about Mr. Craney Crow. He'd walk a little ways, then have to sit down beside the road 'cause he was laughing so hard. Finally he made it as far as Brer Fox's house.

Brer Fox was working in his pea patch. When he heard somebody laughing, he looked over the fence to see who it was. And there was Brer Rabbit rolling around in the grass, holding his sides and laughing.

"Hey, Brer Rabbit! What's the matter with you?"

Brer Rabbit was laughing so hard, he couldn't do nothing but shake his head.

Miz Fox stuck her head out the window. "Sandy, what's all that racket? Don't you know that the baby just went to sleep?"

"It ain't nobody but Brer Rabbit, and it look to me like he got the hysterics."

"Well, I don't care what he got. He better take his racket away from here before he wakes the baby and scares the life out of them what ain't asleep."

Brer Rabbit caught his breath and walked up to the house to pass the time of day with Brer Fox and his wife. "I apologize for all my carrying on," he told them, "but I can't help it. Maybe it ain't right to laugh at them who ain't got the sense they ought to have been born with, but I can't help myself. To tell the truth, I should've been home hours ago, and I would've been if not for something I saw last night." He started laughing again.

"What did you see, Brer Rabbit?" Miz Fox wanted to know. "It sho' sounds like it was funny, and I ain't never turned a good laugh away from my door."

So Brer Rabbit told them all about ol' Craney Crow coming into the Swamp and not knowing how to go to bed. "And the funny thing was that Craney Crow didn't know that when you go to bed, you're supposed to take your head off." Brer Rabbit started laughing again.

Miz Fox looked at Brer Fox. He looked at her, and they didn't know what to say or how to say it.

Brer Rabbit saw how they were looking at each other but didn't let on. "Craney Crow looked like a man who's been around and knows what the fashion is. But when he got to the Swamp and saw all the creatures sleeping with their heads off, he looked like somebody who just came out of the country and seen neon lights for the first time. He stood there with his mouth open like he ain't got no more sense than a crocker sack." Brer Rabbit laughed again. "Well, I been trying to get home all this time to tell my wife about how Craney Crow looked when he seen what the new fashion is."

Brer Rabbit commenced to laughing again. Brer Fox and Miz Fox laughed too. They didn't want Brer Rabbit to think that they were as dumb as Craney Crow.

"Where Craney Crow come from that he don't know the fashion?" Miz Fox asked.

Brer Rabbit shook his head. "He must be from so far back in the country that the Sun don't shine there yet."

Brer Fox said that he didn't much care about fashion, to tell the truth.

Brer Rabbit agreed. "I like the old ways myself. But when something new comes along that makes sense, I ain't gon' turn my back on it just because it's new. No, sir! Before I got in the habit of sleeping with my head off, I wouldn't have believed that it could be so comfortable. The first time I tried it, well, I don't mind telling you I was a little nervous. But I got used to it pretty quick, and now, if it was to go out of fashion, I'd keep right on with it and wouldn't care what nobody thought."

Brer Rabbit looked up at the Sun, which was steadily climbing the arch of heaven, made his farewells, and went on his way.

"Well, that's something, ain't it?" Brer Fox said to his wife. "Sleeping with your head off. I ain't never heard of such a thing."

Miz Fox grunted. "The world ain't big enough to hold all the things you ain't heard of. Here I am scrimping and working my eyeballs out to be as good as the neighbors, and you don't give a hoot if your family is in fashion or not."

"Sleeping with your head off is a fashion I ain't got much interest in trying."

"No, and you ain't got no interest in what folks say about me and the children neither. No wonder Brer Rabbit was laughing so hard. You ought to seen the way your mouth was hanging open when he was telling us about it. I bet he's setting up right now telling his wife about how tacky the Fox family is."

Miz Fox went back in the house. After a while Brer Fox came in to eat breakfast, but the stove looked as cold as a snowball in February. "Ain't you fixing my breakfast this morning?"

"Fixing and eating breakfast is one of the fashions. If you ain't gon' follow the fashions, I don't see how come I should."

Brer Fox went out back of the house and sat down to do some thinking and scratch his fleas. That night when it was time to go to bed, Brer Fox came in. "I reckon I'm ready to get my head taken off so's I can sleep."

Miz Fox was so happy. "I knowed you loved me," she said.

Brer Fox grinned. "But I don't know nothing about how to do it. I reckon you gon' have to help me."

Miz Fox didn't know no more than Brer Fox did, so they sat on the edge of the bed and talked about it for a while.

"You could twist my head off."

"Ticklish as you is, that ain't gon' work."

"What about the ax?"

"That give me the heebie-jeebies."

They sat in silence for a long while until Miz Fox said, "The ax scares me. But on the other hand, we know that if something is the fashion, it ain't gon' hurt."

She went to the woodshed and came back with the ax. "You ready, honey?"

"Ready as I'll ever be," Brer Fox responded.

Whack! Off came his head at the neck. Brer Fox squirmed and twitched and kicked. Miz Fox smiled and said, "That's a sign he's dreaming."

After a while Brer Fox was still. "He look like he having the best sleep he's ever had."

Miz Fox got ready to go to bed and then realized that she still had her head on. She bent over and shook Brer Fox, trying to wake him up so he could help get her head off. She shook him; she hollered at him, but he didn't stir. So she had to go to bed with her head on.

She couldn't sleep for worrying about what the neighbors would think if they knew she was lying in bed with her head on. When she finally got to sleep, she had awful dreams. In one of them Brer Rabbit was laughing at her, and when she made a grab for him, dogs started chasing her. She was glad when morning came.

She went to wake up Brer Fox, but he just lay there. She shook him and yelled at him and pushed him and pulled him. But he just lay there. She started hollering so loud that Brer Rabbit, who was going by on the road, thought she was calling him. He went to the door to see what she wanted.

"Brer Rabbit!" she exclaimed. "I'm sho' glad to see you. I been trying to wake up Brer Fox, and he's lazier this morning than I've ever seen him, and that's saying a lot."

"He'll get up in good time," Brer Rabbit assured her.

"I don't know what you call good time," she insisted. "The Sun's already way up the sky, and he's still asleep. If I'd known that taking your head off would make you sleep like that, I might not have done it."

"What did you say?" Brer Rabbit asked.

"Brer Fox had me take his head off before he went to bed last night."

"What did you take it off with?"

"The ax."

Brer Rabbit covered his mouth with his hands and walked away. It looked like he was crying. But he wasn't. When he got down the road a piece, he started laughing. He laughed so hard, he fell over in the ditch. Like he'd said, some folks didn't have the sense they should've been born with.

The Race

Brer Rabbit went to the Rainmaker's house, which was between Thunder and Lightning and Dark Clouds. Don't nobody know how to get there no more. Folks nowadays need a map to get from one place to another, and where Ol' Rainmaker live at on no map. Where he lived wasn't far and it wasn't near, and if Brer Rabbit had known where he was going, he wouldn't have gotten there.

Rainmaker was storing up water for all the storms he was going to make that year, and he was glad to take a break when Brer Rabbit walked up.

"How you doing, Ol' Rainmaker?"

Ol' Rainmaker allowed as to how he was doing all right. They chatted back and forth for a while, which was the way folks did things back in them days. Finally Brer Rabbit got down to business.

"I was wondering, Ol' Rainmaker, if you could fix up a race between Brer Dust and Cousin Rain to see which one can run the fastest."

Ol' Rainmaker didn't like the idea, and he flashed some lightning and rumbled some thunder while he thought it over. "If anybody but you had come and asked me, Brer Rabbit, I wouldn't do it. Seeing as how it's you, I'll fix it up for you."

Brer Rabbit sent news to all the animals that next Sunday, in the middle of the big road, there was going to be a race.

Sunday came, and all the animals were there. They spread out along the road so they could see the race from start to finish. Brer Bear was at the bend in the road. Brer Fox was at the crossroads. Brer Wolf was at the starting line, and Brer Possum was at the finish line, and the rest were scattered in between.

They waited and waited, and after a while a cloud came floating over. It wasn't a big cloud, but Brer Rabbit knew that Cousin Rain and Uncle Wind were in it. The cloud dropped down slowly until it was right over the road, and then it settled slowly to the ground. Cousin Rain and Uncle Wind got out and went to the starting line. Of course, Brer Dust was already there.

Brer Rabbit fired the starting gun, and they were off! Uncle Wind didn't mean to, but he was as much help to Brer Dust as he was to Cousin Rain 'cause he blew and blew, and Brer Dust whirled up, and before any of the animals knew anything, there was dust everywhere. Brer Coon was holding on to Brer Bear to keep from getting blowed away, but Miz Partridge was blown halfway to Mr. Sun's summer place on Lake Gimme a Break. All the animals were covered with so much dust, they looked like sand dunes.

Then Cousin Rain got going. If the animals were miserable being turned into sand dunes, they had the double misery when Cousin Rain made 'em into mud dunes. Of course Brer Rabbit had had a raincoat and umbrella hidden away and put 'em on when the race started. He was dry as a rock in the desert.

The animals got so mad they forgot all about the race and set out after Brer Rabbit, and he outran Brer Dust and Cousin Rain and he wasn't even supposed to be in the race.

As for who won the real race, well, it turned out this way: Cousin Rain thought she had lost. Brer Dust had put so much dust in the air that she hadn't been able to see a thing.

"Where you at, Brer Dust? You done crossed the finish line?"

Brer Dust hollered back, "I fell down in the mud and can't run no more."

So Cousin Rain was the winner.

APPENDIX

Appendix for *The Tales of Uncle Remus: The Adventures of Brer Rabbit* (Vol. I) and *More Tales of Uncle Remus: Further Adventures of Brer Rabbit, His Friends, Enemies, and Others* (Vol. II)

The following separate stories were combined into single stories:

"The Wonderful Tar-Baby Story" and "How Mr. Rabbit Was Too Sharp for Mr. Fox" became "Brer Rabbit and the Tar Baby" (Vol. I).

"Mr. Rabbit Grossly Deceives Mr. Fox," "Mr. Fox Is Again Victimized," and "Mr. Fox Is Outdone by Mr. Buzzard" became "Brer Rabbit Gets Even" (Vol. I).

"Brother Rabbit and His Famous Foot" and "Brother Rabbit Submits to a Test" became "Brer Rabbit's Luck" (Vol. I).

"Mr. Man Has Some Meat" and "Brother Rabbit Gets the Meat" became "Brer Rabbit Gets the Meat" (Vol. II).

"How Craney-Crow Lost His Head" and "Brother Fox Follows the Fashion" became "Being Fashionable Ain't Always Healthy" (Vol. II).

The following Brer Rabbit stories of Joel Chandler Harris were omitted from these two volumes (See Introduction, Vol. I):

"Brother Rabbit Gets the Provisions"
"Cutta Cord-La!"
"Brother Fox and the White Muscadines"
"Mr. Hawk and Brother Rabbit"
"Brother Fox Makes a Narrow Escape"
"Brother Fox's Fish Trap"
"Brother Rabbit and the Gingercakes"
"Brother Rabbit and Miss Nancy"
"Brer Rabbit's Frolic"
"Brer Rabbit and the Gold Mine"
"How Brer Rabbit Saved Brer B'ar's Life"
"Brother Rabbit's Bear Hunt"
"Taily-Po"
"Brother Rabbit, Brother Fox, and Two Fat Pullets"
"How Brother Rabbit Brought Family Trouble on Brother Fox"

BIBLIOGRAPHY

Afro-American Folktales: Stories from Black Traditions in the New World. Selected and edited by Roger D. Abrahams. Pantheon Books, New York, 1985.
  This is an important collection of black folktales from an important folklorist.

"The Trickster in Relation to Greek Mythology," by Károly Kerényi in *The Trickster: A Study in American Indian Mythology,* by Paul Radin. Philosophical Library. New York, 1956.

"On the Psychology of the Trickster Figure," by C. G. Jung in the work cited above.

The Zande Trickster, edited by E. E. Evans-Pritchard. Oxford University Press, London, 1967.

Julius Lester is the critically acclaimed author of books for both children and adults. His latest book for Dial, *The Tales of Uncle Remus: The Adventures of Brer Rabbit*, is an *American Bookseller* Pick of the Lists. Other books for Dial include *To Be a Slave*, a Newbery Medal Honor Book; *Long Journey Home: Stories from Black History*, a National Book Award finalist; *This Strange New Feeling*; and *The Knee-High Man and Other Tales*, an American Library Association *Notable Book, School Library Journal* Best Book of the Year, and Lewis Carroll Shelf Award Winner. His adult books include *Do Lord Remember Me*, a *New York Times* Notable Book, and *Lovesong: Becoming a Jew*.

The son of a Methodist minister, Mr. Lester was born in St. Louis. At fourteen he moved to Nashville, where he later received his Bachelor of Arts from Fisk University. He is married and is the father of four children. He lives in Amherst and teaches at the University of Massachusetts.

Jerry Pinkney has twice received the Coretta Scott King Award for Illustration, first for the Dial book *The Patchwork Quilt*, written by Valerie Flournoy. *The Patchwork Quilt* also won the Christopher Award, was an American Library Association *Notable Book,* a *Booklist* Reviewers' Choice, and a Reading Rainbow selection. Mr. Pinkney has illustrated many other books, including *Song of the Trees* for Dial, written by Mildred D. Taylor. His artwork has been shown at the 1986 Bologna Book Fair, the AIGA Book Show, the Society of Illustrators Annual Show, and in museums around the country.

Mr. Pinkney studied at the Philadelphia Museum College of Art. He and his wife, who have four grown children, live in Croton-on-Hudson, New York.